A NOTE FROM P. J. HOOVER

BACK IN HIGH SCHOOL, I WAS FIRST INTRODUCED TO THE *Odyssey*. I'd always been a fan of mythology, but there was something about this particular story that stuck with me. For me, though, the story was a fun adventure tale with lots of scary monsters. And sure, scary monsters are great, but they aren't enough to explain a story staying popular for thousands of years.

In 2008, I was at a book festival in Oklahoma. Sitting next to me during the book signings was a friendly, chatty author, and we soon got on the subject of mythology. In addition to talking about our favorite myths, I expressed my fascination with this crazy story I loved, *The Odyssey*.

"Oh, *The Odyssey*. It's a great story," he said. "But have you ever heard of the poem *Ithaka* by Constantine P. Cavafy? I think you would love it."

Of course, I hadn't heard of the poem. But once I got back to Austin, I quickly looked it up.

And read it.

And printed it out.

And read it again.

And I discovered this layer of *The Odyssey* that I never knew anything about. I'd been tricked in high school. This wasn't just a story about monsters. This was a story about a hero facing new challenges, trying to save his men, failing over and over, reaching his lowest point, and still pushing on. It was never about him getting to Ithaka. It was always about the journey and how he changed while on it.

Homer's Excellent Adventure is the story of my heart. It's the story of me facing my own challenges, failing many times, and finally succeeding. It's the story of every kid. It's the story of all of us.

ADVANCE PRAISE FOR HOMER'S EXCELLENT ADVENTURE

"Homer's Excellent Adventure *is a wonderful retelling of* The Odyssey . . . *students will appreciate as they enjoy this cultural icon in an easy read that will have them laughing out loud. And likely begging for 'more like this one!'"*
—Dorcas Hand, AASL Award Committee Chair

"Homer *felt like a comic adventure retelling of* The Odyssey *with lots of action, wit and wisdom thrown in. I read this book in one day because I could NOT put it down."*
—Ginna Hill, Librarian, Fern Bluff Elementary School

"When it comes to Mythology Mash-ups, no one does it quite like P. J. Hoover! Her ability to take a classic and make it her own is beyond amazing! Give this book to your geeks, to your bookworms and to your reluctant readers. It is a sure to be a hit!!"*
—Margie Longoria, Texas TAYSHAS Reading List

"Homer's Excellent Adventure *is just what young readers need to get them hooked on the stories of ancient Greece. I loved the idea of getting to know Homer as a character and the novelty of him as a participant in Odysseus' journeys! Treat yourself to this fun twist on Homer's classic!"*
—Cindi Rockett, Librarian, Trinity High School

"What a fun story! I loved the friendship bond between Homer and Dory. Their travels through history were exciting and informative . . . I can't wait to see where their future adventures take us!"*
—Jennifer Kirby, Cooper Elementary Librarian

HOMER'S
EXCELLENT
ADVENTURE

P. J. HOOVER

CBAY Books
Dallas, Texas

For Kay and Morgan, for listening to the story over and over again.

TABLE OF CONTENTS

Upside Down in the Hands of a Giant 1

From the Beginning. 4

Falafels with the Gods 14

Into the Horse. 23

As You Set Out for Ithaca. 37

It all Starts with One Bad Choice 44

Flower Children 58

Into the Cave. 75

Dinner for the Cyclops 84

Cloaked in Mutton 93

The Rainbow Sparkle Club 97

Skeletons in the Closet 109

Cheeseburger in Paradise. 120

Going Porcine 122

Strange Brew. 133

Standing on the Beach 140

It's the Edge of the World as We Know It 144

Two Tickets for Paradise 150

Same Song, Second Verse. 163

Siren's Song. 171

Don't Stop Believing 176

The Sad Parts 185

Warnings of the Dead. 187

Peaches and Cream 192

Walking on Sunshine 199

Spin Me Right Round. 210

Greek Letters. 216

A Heroic Divergence 218

The Coconut Owl 228

Blinded by the Light 234

Lost But Not Forgotten 236

Tales of Brave Ulysses. 242

A Farewell to Kings 255

The Mark Is the Secret 262

This Is the End. 272

GLOSSARY 276

MAP 283

HOMER'S SUPER SIMPLE GUIDE TO
     DACTYLIC HEXAMETER 284

DORY'S RECIPES: THE TASTIEST HARDTACK
     IN THE (ANCIENT) WORLD. 288

"Tell me, O muse, of that ingenious hero who travelled far and wide after he had sacked the famous town of Troy."

— Homer, *The Odyssey*

UPSIDE DOWN IN THE HANDS OF A GIANT

DON'T MAKE THE GODS ANGRY. I KNOW THIS FROM firsthand experience. Making the gods angry was completely the reason why I was upside down, dangling from the hands of a cyclops with every drop of blood rushing to my brain. Actually, if I had even half a brain, I wouldn't be in this position in the first place. I'd be back in Ionia, milking cows with Mom. Every twelve-year-old boy's dream, I know. But it sure beat my current situation.

"You're not going to be able to start the story there, Homer," Dory interrupted. "You're skipping all kinds of stuff."

I tried to focus on my best friend's words, but my head still reeled from this secret I'd found out about Dory earlier today. I could never tell anyone. Odysseus would have blown a gasket if he'd found out. But that wasn't my issue right now. My issue was the cyclops.

Dory dangled next to me. We were totally hosed. From down on the ground, I heard Odysseus and a few of the not-so-smart guys yelling up at us. The smarter ones kept quiet and hid in the dark recesses of the cave.

"Where should I start the story? Back at the horse?" I asked. Not that I was writing any of this down at the moment. I couldn't reach my scroll or my pen.

"Not back at the horse. That's not even kind of the beginning." The look Dory gave me made me sure I was about to get smacked upside my head.

"It is," I said. "It's where we met Odysseus."

Dory's spikey dark hair shook from side to side, looking a lot like upside-down grass growing from the sky, exposing a neck inked with a tattoo I'd never notice before. Dory covered it quickly with a hand. "Before that. Back in Ionia."

"Ionia!" I said. "That place was so freaking boring." Not that I'd mind a little boring right now.

I guess I spoke a little too loudly because the cyclops—Polyphemus was his name—started shaking me. My teeth rattled around in my mouth, and I'm pretty sure my brains were turning to jelly. I watched as my scroll and pen fell from my pockets. I guess I wouldn't miss them if Polyphemus decided to eat me.

"Boring, maybe," Dory said. "But it's where the story starts. And you can't start a story in the middle."

"Why not?" I lowered my voice, hoping good old Poly

2

would decide I wasn't worth any effort and would toss me aside. Maybe he'd nibble on my finger and think I tasted bad.

"Duh," Dory said. "Because you'll confuse people. They won't understand anything about why you're on the adventure. And if they don't understand why you're on the adventure, they won't *care* why you're on the adventure. They'll stop listening. And that, my friend, is the death of a storyteller."

"I think I'm already a dead storyteller," I said as Polyphemus lifted me closer to his gaping mouth. It was so gross. There were pieces of flesh trapped between his brown teeth. And I knew they were fresh, because he'd just eaten a couple of Odysseus' guys earlier. I don't know their real names, but one of them we called Spitter since he always used to spit on his food so no one else would touch it.

"Just trust me, Homer," Dory said. "Start from the beginning."

The beginning. The end. What did it matter? My death loomed before me.

"Fine," I said. "From the beginning."

FROM THE BEGINNING

RIGHT . . . SO THE STORY . . . IT STARTS IN IONIA, JUST
like Dory said. I sat on my bench in school. It wasn't a real
school. Just a reclaimed barn that used to belong to the royal
family but then got re-purposed for the good of the people. It
still smelled like a barn, and there were smears of pig dung on
the wooden walls that I had to scrub every time I got detention.

There I was, struggling through another endless day of
boring math and spelling and science. I had no idea why any
of this stuff mattered for becoming a soldier, but rules were
rules, so I had to be here. I tried to keep my eyes open as our
teacher, Elder Pachis, droned on and on about language arts of
all things. No subject was more boring. Except maybe history.
That was pretty awful, too. Heat poured through the windows,
like the gods were testing me to see how much I could stand

before falling asleep.

Apparently not much because, as hard as I tried, my eyes would not stay open. I used my fingertips to prop my lids open, but that didn't work. I pinched myself like fifty times. I counted the wrinkles on Elder Pachis' face. Halfway through, I lost count, so I started again. But then I couldn't take it any longer. I finally drifted off. I was having some amazing dream about being the head of the royal guard and living in the palace with piles of fresh fruit and meat cooked to perfection. Music played in the background. Someone walked up and offered to rub my feet.

"Of course," I said, swaying with the music.

"Of course what?" a voice answered that was way more harsh than seemed right for the dream.

"Of course ..." My thoughts slipped away from me. What had I been talking about?

"Homer," the voice said again.

I struggled to open my eyes, but in the dream, they wouldn't budge.

"Mmmm ...," I said.

Crack. My hand exploded in pain.

I opened my mouth to scream but stopped myself as the real world returned around me. Elder Pachis hovered over me. He held an ivory ruler in his right hand, which must've been what just hit my hand. A quick glance down showed a bright red welt forming.

"Having trouble staying awake, are we?" he cackled.

5

Ugh, this guy. He had to be the worst teacher in the universe. If he bothered to say anything interesting, maybe I'd have wanted to listen. But come on. For the last hour he'd been explaining story arc. I was confused for most of it since it took me that long to figure out he wasn't talking about a big boat.

"I wasn't asleep," I said, shoving a piece of my shaggy hair out of my face.

The entire class laughed.

"You were snoring," Demetrios said. He was this snotty rich kid who made fun of my dreams of being a soldier every chance he got. He was like my polar opposite: wavy dark hair, super buff. All the girls fawned all over him. Me? My blond hair always looked like I'd been caught in a hurricane, even though I swear I brushed it, and despite soldier training and working on a farm, I could barely make a muscle.

"And drooling," Lysandra said, tossing her red hair over her shoulder as she laughed.

Yeah, she was Demetrios' girlfriend. And fine, I had a huge crush on her since the first day of school, even though she never said more than two words to me at a time. Also, those two words normally made me want to crawl under a bench. Kind of like right now.

"See me after class, Homer," Elder Pachis said.

I knew what staying after school meant. Aside from scrubbing pig dung off the walls, I'd be tracing on the dirt floor, over and over again, *I will not fall asleep during class.* It only made me want to fall asleep that much more.

"Oooh …," Demetrios said. "Homer is in trouble."

I wanted to punch him.

I didn't because it would upset Mom if she found out. Also, it could get me kicked out of school. And no education meant no being a soldier like my dad. Of course, Mom wouldn't be too upset about this last part. She didn't want me to be a soldier, and she refused to let me mention it since that was how Dad had died. Well, she said he was dead. I wasn't willing to give up on him even though he'd been missing for two years.

Fear of drooling kept me awake for the rest of the day. After everyone else filed out of the smelly school, I shuffled my feet and wandered up to the front of the classroom.

"I've given you lots of chances, Homer," Elder Pachis said.

"Yeah, I was up super late—" I started, ready to defend myself like normal. We went through this every time I got in trouble. Old Man Pachis lectured me. I listened and nodded and then scrubbed the walls and wrote words in the dirt.

"But no more chances," he said, stopping my words.

I must've heard wrong.

"What do you mean, no more chances?" There were always more chances. This had to be at least the twentieth time I'd gotten in trouble.

He waggled his finger and eyebrows in sync. "Well, what I mean is that you don't get any more chances."

My heart started pounding. This was not how our conversation went.

"Okay," I said. "So what, then? You want me to clean better

around here this time? You want me to sweep?"

"No. No. No," Elder Pachis said. "You aren't listening. I said no more chances. The rules say I can't give you any more."

"And …," I said.

"And that's it. You're out of school."

Out of school? He couldn't be serious.

"You can't be serious," I said.

"I'm completely serious," Elder Pachis said. He pointed at himself. "Look at this face. Do I look like I'm kidding?"

I looked at his face. It was covered in forty-two wrinkles (as of my earlier count) and reminded me of old sandal leather. It also didn't look like it was kidding. It actually looked a little sad to be delivering such grim news, almost like Elder Pachis had a heart inside his withered chest.

"But that can't be it," I said. At this point, my heart pounded so hard, it was making huge whooshing noises in my ears, like I was in the middle of a giant tunnel with nothing else around.

"It can be," Elder Pachis said. "It is. I've let you off as many times as I'm allowed. School's over for you."

I stood there as his words sunk in. The only thing I'd ever wanted in life was to be a soldier like my dad, and that dream was slipping away. And then there was Mom. I was never going to be able to go home again. The idea of facing her, of disappointing her … It was too much. I could almost see her face fall. See the tears slip from her eyes. Here I was, her only son, and I was a huge failure in life. The worst son possible.

"But what about being a soldier?" I said.

Elder Pachis shook his head. "Not without an education."

"So I'm supposed to go home and work on the farm for the rest of my life?" I could hardly say the words.

"Well …," Elder Pachis said. "The farm won't be able to belong to you and your mother anymore. With no adult male in the household and the only son no longer being a valid student, the farm will be repossessed by the state."

"Repossessed!"

"By the mayor," Elder Pachis said.

That made it even worse. The mayor was Demetrios' dad. No way in all the realm of Hades was I going to go groveling to their family. They already treated me and Mom like cow dung, ever since Dad hadn't come home. Hardly better than slaves.

"But Elder Pachis—"

"Save your excuses," Elder Pachis said. "It won't do any good. I can't do anything else."

The whole world seemed to collapse around me. It was like watching my life get flushed down a whirlpool. But not just my life. Mom's life, too. Without our farm, we would have nowhere to go. No relatives. Mom would have to live off the mercy of others forever. I could not let that happen.

"One more chance," I pleaded. "Please."

Elder Pachis set his ruler down on his desk and met my eyes. We stood there, face to wrinkled face. I tried to keep my lips from quivering even though every part of me wanted to keep begging him for my future.

"Homer," he finally said, "why should I give you one

more chance?"

I shuffled through my memories, like grains of sand on the beach. There was nothing I could find. No reason I could come up with that had any merit. I'd hated school. Been the worst of students. But right now, there was nothing I wanted so much as to stay here forever.

"Because I really need it." I bit my tongue to keep from saying any more. "It means everything to me."

I could almost see the sun move across the sky as the seconds ticked by. But I couldn't back down now. This was it. The moment of truth.

"Have you started your assignment yet?" Elder Pachis asked.

"Assignment?" I asked, trying not to cringe as the word came out. But not remembering some assignment wasn't making me look any better.

"Your semester project," he said.

"Semester project?" I said, even though I was starting to sound like a parrot. "Which semester project are you talking about specifically?"

Elder Pachis clenched his fists like he was trying to control a lifetime of annoyances that ran through him. I hoped his giant knuckles didn't pop from the effort. "The one I assigned three days ago."

I nodded my head even though I had no clue what he was talking about.

He grabbed something off his desk. I swear it hadn't been there a second before. It was a tightly wound scroll held together by a leather tie. He grasped it between both of his gnarled hands.

"There might be one way we can get around the rules, Homer," he said. "You know what I need?"

Elder Pachis needed a day at the spa. Some sunscreen. Maybe fifty years off his life. But I bit back my normal witty replies.

"What?" I asked.

He whapped the scroll into his palm. "I need a story."

"A story?"

"A story."

"What kind of story?" I asked, hoping he didn't think I was messing with him because I totally wasn't. Hadn't he just been yammering on about stories for the last three hours?

"A story to fill this scroll," he said. "And I'll make you a deal. If you can get me that story as your semester project, then I'll find a way to give you one last chance."

My heart pounded. He wanted me, his worst student, to write a story for him? It was impossible. But it was also the only chance I was ever going to get of saving Mom, me, the farm, and my future.

"I'll do it," I said, reaching for the scroll.

He pulled it out of reach. "It must be an amazing story," he said. "Filled with fantastical adventures. Epic heroes. It must be a story of legend. Something never seen before. A story that will last for all the ages."

I gulped. He completely had the wrong guy for this task. I

11

wasn't a storyteller. I didn't even like writing.

But no. I was not going to let that sway me.

"No problem," I said, trying again for the scroll.

"I'm serious, Homer," Elder Pachis said. "This is your only chance. If you don't fill this scroll with the most epic story ever, then you may never set foot in this school again. Your farm will be taken away. You'll never be a soldier. You and your mother will be out on the streets. So, what do you say?"

My mind screamed at me to run away. To pinch myself until I woke up from this horrible nightmare. I could not believe I'd let myself get into this situation in the first place. Still, I had no choice.

I nodded my head and plastered a smile on my face. "I am totally up for the job," I said, holding my hand out for the scroll. "I'll write you the best story in the universe."

"It has to have an arc," Elder Pachis said.

I nodded. He was not talking about a boat.

"And character growth."

I kept on nodding. People grew all the time. I'd grown five inches in the last six months.

"And motivation," Elder Pachis said. "All these things make up a great story."

"I'm on it," I said. Between Mom, my dreams of being a soldier, and keeping the farm, I was loaded to the eyebrows with motivation.

"And the project is due in ten days," Elder Pachis said. "If yours is even an hour late, it's as good as a failure."

I held out the hourglass I wore on a chain around my neck. Dad gave it to me before he went out for his last campaign. He told me I should use it to count the days until he got back. Except when the other soldiers returned, he wasn't with them. I'd stopped counting two years ago.

"No way will it be late," I said. Ten days was plenty of time to write a story. Ten turns of the hourglass. That was forever.

Elder Pachis eyed me once more and finally handed me the scroll. I flipped the hourglass, resetting it, to make sure we were starting at the same time.

"Oh, and one final thing," he said.

"Anything."

"It must be in Dactylic Hexameter."

"No problem," I said. I had no idea what that was, but I'd figure it out. How hard could it be?

Falafels with the Gods

I SHOVED THE SCROLL INTO MY TUNIC AND GRABBED a reed pen and some ink from the supply shelf and then high-tailed it out of there. I had to get on with finding my story. I could write about this whole stupid school experience. Now that was a story. And I'd finish it with me handing this dumb scroll filled out completely back to Elder Pachis. He'd be so impressed by my story that I'd watch as tears rolled down his cheeks. It would be my moment of glory.

But I wasn't a block out of school when the smell of falafels wafted over to me. Man, I loved me some falafel.

I wandered into the plaza and over to my favorite falafel cart. There were only four stools, three of which were already occupied. The two barstools on the right were taken by these two guys who always came after their work shift at the manure

14

factory. They smelled like dung and had so many missing teeth, I figured the only thing they could eat was falafel. On the third barstool was some teenager with curly brown hair wearing a hat and tattered clothes that looked like he'd just wandered in from a traveling caravan.

I plunked down on the fourth barstool—the one on the far left.

"Sup, Homer," the kid behind the serving bar said. He had spikey dark hair that came to his shoulders, light skin, and super long eyelashes that made his dark green eyes seem really huge. He was also the closest thing I had to a best friend.

"Sup, Dory," I said.

Dory ran the falafel cart. Not for himself. That would actually be super cool. I could see the fun in that kind of life, making falafels all day long. But no, Dory was a slave. His master—yep, you got it: Demetrios' dad—owned the falafel cart. He just made Dory run it for him since Dory was pretty good at cooking.

"Slow day today," Dory said, shoving a hot falafel in front of me. He never asked for cash. When I could, I'd bring along special treats from the farm to give him in exchange. But with this whole disaster at school, I'd completely forgotten to stop by home and get anything.

"Great," I said, picking at the falafel. But now, with it here in front of me, I realized that I wasn't all that hungry. I had bigger things on my mind. "You can help me with something."

"Sure, watcha got?" Dory said, wiping his greasy hands all over the front of his green apron. Once, I'd made the mistake of watching how much olive oil he put into the falafels. It had taken me a whole week to eat another one. But I'd pushed past the gross factor, because falafels were worth it.

"A project at school. I need a story to fill this." I pulled the scroll from my tunic. My thumb left a huge splotch of grease on the scroll. I tried to wipe it, but that just made the grease stain smear even more. But Elder Pachis had never said anything about the scroll looking nice. It just needed a story.

An amazing story.

Within ten days.

His words rushed back to me with a haunting swiftness. I had to do this. Everything was at stake. I could never face Mom again if I failed. I could never go home. And I'd never be in the army.

Dory took a step back and looked at the scroll like it might bite him. "You know I can't read or write, Homer."

That's right. Aside from having no freedom and not being able to own any property, slaves in Ionia weren't allowed to read or write. Demetrios' dad claimed it might make them too powerful, and then they'd revolt.

I put up my hands. "That's okay. I can. You can just help me come up with the story. You're good with stories and ideas."

Dory looked at me like I'd confused him with someone else. "No, I'm not."

"You totally are," I said. "Remember last week when you were telling me about how you spiced the soup? How Demetrios turned bright red and started crying? That was so

16

funny. I was crying."

"That story was like two minutes long," Dory said. "It wasn't even a story."

"It was awesome," I said, even though now that I thought about it, I could see that he was right. A story about spiced soup wasn't going to get me the second chance I needed with Elder Pachis.

"What about that story you told about setting the falafel cart on fire?" I said. "You smothered the fire with Demetrios' new coat. Man, I loved that story."

Dory grinned. "Okay, that actually was pretty funny. But your teacher might not think so. That coat probably cost more than what he makes in a year."

"Hmm …," I said. "You're probably right. But you can help me think of something."

"What kind of story do you need?" the guy at the barstool next to me asked.

I turned to look at him. He was a teenager, like I thought, probably only four or five years older than me or Dory, with scruffy brown hair wound into curls so tight he could have stored pencils in them. Maybe he had a story he could tell me.

"Do I know you?" I asked because he looked kind of familiar.

"Do you?" the guy said.

"I'm Homer," I said.

I expected him to tell me his name next. That's what any polite person might have done. But instead, he just said, "Homer. That works."

"Works for what?"

"It has a nice ring to it," he said.

"Glad you approve." I wasn't sure why this guy cared how my name sounded. My name was my name. It wasn't like I planned to change it if some teenager didn't think it rolled off the tongue nicely.

"So, Homer," the guy said. "What kind of story do you need?"

"Just something for school," I said. "It's no big deal."

"Really?"

Yeah, not really. Just saying it made the complete horror of my situation come back to me. It was a big deal. And I needed help.

So, I told him and Dory all about my trouble at school and everything Elder Pachis had said and the ten days and the scroll. And as I recounted the error of my ways, I realized with complete certainty the trouble I'd gotten myself into. This was the kind of story I was never going to find. And even if through some ridiculous means I managed to find this kind of story, I knew nothing about story telling. If I tried to write it down, it wouldn't even be worth the cost of the papyrus. I might as well use it in the outhouse to wipe.

Dory and the guy listened until I was done. I picked at my falafel a little bit more even though I'd completely lost my appetite.

"So you need an epic story," the guy said. "An excellent adventure."

I nodded. "That pretty much sums it up."

18

"Nothing exciting happens in Ionia," Dory said, further confirming my certain failure.

"True that," the guy said.

"You guys are no help at all, you know that?" I grabbed the scroll and tightened it. My other fingers left grease stains too, but I didn't care. I was going to have to go home to Mom and break the bad news. Maybe we could move to a mountain cave or something. Live off the land—as long as bandits didn't find and kill us.

"I can help," the guy said.

"Yeah, whatever."

"No really," he said. "You think it's just a coincidence that I'm sitting here right now?"

I glanced around the marketplace. There were at least ten other food trailers, most with a couple empty seats.

"You said you liked the falafels," Dory said, putting his hands on his hips.

"They are pretty good, but they're not the reason I'm here."

I crossed my arms. I didn't know if this guy could tell or not, but I was not in the mood for joking today. "Just spit out whatever you're trying to say, okay?"

"Sure," the guy said. He placed a hand on his chest and kind of gave a half bow. "I am Hermes, messenger of the gods."

I glanced to Dory, and we both busted out laughing.

"What?" the guy said.

"You expect us to believe you're Hermes?" I said.

He nodded.

"You're a god?" Dory said.

"Yep."

"You?"

"Why is that so hard to believe?" the guy said.

"Because you look like a teenager," I said.

The guy who was pretending to be Hermes smirked. "That's because I want to look like a teenager. But check this out." And as we watched, the silly little hat sitting on his head transformed, and two white wings grew from the sides of it. His skin brightened, almost like he was covered in golden glitter. And his smile widened, showing off perfect teeth that the two guys sitting next to him would have killed for.

"Oh my gods," I said. "You weren't lying."

"Of course I'm not lying," Hermes said.

"You're sparkling," Dory said.

"You think it's too much?" Hermes asked, looking down at his arm.

"Just a little," I said, and the glitter factor on his skin lowered back down to a simmer.

"I don't know," Dory said. "I kind of like the sparkle."

"What about the hat?" Hermes said, smoothing the wings back.

"The wings are pretty cool," Dory said. "But that hat is so last century."

"Whatever," Hermes said, and the wings and sparkle faded away. "What I'm trying to tell you is that I am a god, and I can help you with this whole story thing."

A small spark of hope ignited inside me. What if Hermes was telling the truth? What if he really could help me?

"You can tell me a story?" I asked, knowing my eyes had probably grown as wide as the Ionian gold coins with King Telamon's face on them.

"Of course not," Hermes said. "I'm not telling you a story."

"But you just said—"

"I said I could help you."

"How?" I asked.

"How many days did you say you had?" Hermes asked.

I pulled the hourglass out from under my tunic. "Ten," I said, holding it out.

Hermes reached forward and grasped the hourglass in his hand.

"My dad gave me that," I said, wanting to pull it back from him but also not wanting him to change his mind and not help me.

But Hermes released it, letting it fall against my chest. It felt really warm, like it had been left next to the fire for a little too long.

"It's a nice hourglass," Hermes said, and then he dug into his pocket and pulled something out. He set it on the bar in front of me and Dory. It was tiny wooden horse, not even as tall as my hand. It had legs, but it also had four wheels like it was some kind of kid's pull toy. There was small door on the side of the horse, like a little compartment or something.

"Oh, a toy," Dory said. "I love toys."

"What's inside?" I asked, as Hermes flipped the door open.

He lifted it up and held it out. Dory and I both leaned forward and peeked into the tiny horse. Something reached from inside the horse and grabbed us, yanking me off my barstool and through the impossible opening.

INTO THE HORSE

"GODS, WHAT'S THAT SMELL?" DORY SAID.

Gone was the delicious scent of deep fried falafel. Instead, it reeked of weeks old body odor combined with fresh sweat.

"Silence!" a gruff voice whispered. A voice that definitely belonged to a grown-up man, not a kid like Dory and me.

I don't know what had happened, but we were no longer at the food trailer. Instead, wherever we were was pitch black. And moving, bumping along like it was being pulled. Small gaps in the surrounding walls let flickering light through, illuminating the space around me enough so I could see silhouettes in the dark.

The voice left no room for discussion. I snapped my mouth shut and prayed that Dory did the same.

He didn't.

"Homer?" he whispered from next to me.

"Right here," I said, feeling for his arm.

"Where are we?" he said.

"No idea."

The cart or whatever it was continued to roll, and the falafel started moving around funny in my stomach, making me seasick. I was not going to retch. Not that it would matter if I did. It might even make the place smell better.

"No talking," the gruff voice said again. "We're almost there."

I had no clue where *there* was. But I also could tell that it wasn't a good idea to ask.

The cart bumped along and finally came to a stop. And then this huge crowd that I couldn't see because they were outside started cheering. It was like a party or something, and music played, and there were screams and laughs and all sorts of celebrating like the yearly Ionia Day parade King Telamon sponsored.

I guess the guy who told us to shut up figured no one would hear us now if we started talking. Or at least if he started talking.

"Here's the plan," the guy said. I still couldn't see his face, but from the sound of his voice, he sat right across from us.

Dory edged closer to me but didn't say a word.

"The celebrating should go all throughout the night," the guy said. "And then, once things quiet down, we climb out, open the gates, and attack."

Attack? I had no clue what this guy was talking about.

"I say we attack now, Odysseus," some guy with a whiny

voice said.

I had no idea how to spell the name that he said, but it sounded like O-D-C-Us. I could work out that detail later.

"We're not attacking now," the guy, who must be named Odysseus, said.

"But if we go right now, they'll never even notice us," the whiny-voiced guy said.

"No, Eurylochus," Odysseus said. It sounded like Yur-E-Lo-Cus.

"But—" he started.

"Don't question me again," Odysseus said. "We wait until they fall asleep. Then, we attack."

And with that, the conversation was over.

A couple of the smelly guys with us in the cart started snoring. One of them let out a giant fart in his sleep. The already rank odor in the cart doubled. I tried not to gag.

Five minutes went by. Then ten. Finally, I couldn't keep quiet any longer.

"Who are we attacking?" I asked Dory.

"What did you say?" the Odysseus guy asked. Guess he wasn't asleep. But now seemed as good a time as any to figure out what was going on. I couldn't really see myself taking a snooze.

"I asked who we're attacking," I said.

"Where have you been the last ten years?" he said.

Elder Pachis always said there was no such thing as a stupid question, but I guess I'd just asked one. Whatever the answer,

I hadn't learned it stuck back in Ionia in the boring classroom.

"I'm just a little confused," I said.

More like a lot confused, and it was only getting worse by the second. I was supposed to be eating falafels.

"Ah, that happens before a great battle," Odysseus said. "Nervous energy. You need to learn to control it."

"I will," I said. "I promise. Just catch me up to speed if you don't mind."

"We're attacking the Trojans, of course," Odysseus said.

I'd heard of the Trojans. I was pretty sure they used to live across the sea or something like that. Elder Pachis had droned on about their downfall at one point. It seemed like the kind of thing I'd fallen asleep during. Now I was kind of wishing I'd paid more attention.

"Why are we attacking the Trojans?" Dory asked.

"Because they're scum!" someone else in the cart bellowed. "Their coward prince, Paris, stole Helen right out from under the nose of King Menelaus. Stole her away. Tried to keep her for himself."

"Did she have a choice in the matter?" Dory asked. "Maybe she liked Paris. Maybe she wanted to go with him."

I elbowed Dory to make him shut up.

"Of course, she didn't want anything to do with that Trojan filth," the guy said. "And for her honor and the honor of King Menelaus, we fight."

"We fight!" another guy echoed. "And near as I can tell, that time has come."

He was right. All the partying noises had simmered down to nothing. Which didn't make me all that happy. Sure, I wanted to be a soldier, but an entire war over some girl seemed borderline ridiculous.

"On my mark, we move," Odysseus said.

"I'm not attacking anyone," Dory whispered.

I had no plans to, either. In every single practice fight during soldier training classes, I'd gotten my butt kicked. If it were up to me, I'd call off the war and join the Trojans for their party.

"Just stay back," I said.

The words were barely out of my mouth when this little side door of the cart we were crammed into flew open. Firelight flooded the inside, as did fresh air. Now that I could see our companions, the reason for the horrific scent became clear. There were five big sweaty guys with beards and long hair that looked like it hadn't been washed in years.

"Attack!" Odysseus said, announcing his battle plans to the world. He was obviously their leader because they all grabbed the hilts of their swords and jumped after him as he dropped out the side of the cart.

I peeked out to see them running back in the direction from where we'd come, screaming and lighting fires as they went.

"What do you think we should do?" I asked Dory.

Outside the cart, a bunch of people slept in the streets, despite all the noise Odysseus and his guys were making. There was trash and all sorts of empty bottles scattered everywhere making it pretty clear they'd been drinking more than juice.

Dory leaned out next to me but then sat back really fast onto his butt.

"Whoa," he said.

"What's up?"

He pointed down. "Did you see how high up we are?"

I leaned back out because the height didn't bother me. We were a good twenty feet in the air, but the crazy thing was that when I looked down, there were wooden horse legs below us. I craned my head upward. Yep, there was a horse head, painted bright gold. We were inside of a colossal wooden horse.

"Hermes did this," I said. "The horse toy. We're inside it."

"We're inside a toy?" Dory said. "That doesn't make a lot of sense, Homer."

I shook my head. "Not inside the toy. Life size, but like the toy. We're inside a giant wooden horse."

"A giant wooden horse?" Dory said.

It didn't make a whole heck of a lot of sense to me either.

A bunch of yelling and screaming came from off in the distance. I guess Odysseus and his men had woken up the Trojans. The attack had begun.

"I got it, Homer! We should stay here," Dory said. "You can work on the story. This is why Hermes sent us here. He probably thinks you should write about this battle. Quick, get the scroll out."

It almost sounded like a good idea, except then, the tallest building that I could see from the giant horse burst into flames. Then, the one in front of that caught fire. And then the next. And the fact that we were in a wooden horse was not lost on me. Firelight reflected off the golden paint. This was not the place to be during a raging fire.

"We need to go," I said to Dory.

He didn't even look out. "I'm staying here."

I grabbed his arm. "Seriously. We need to go now."

Dory only shook his head.

I yanked on his arm, and he yanked back, and we weren't getting anywhere, and the flames were getting closer. Heat poured off them and came toward us in waves.

This was not how I wanted to die. This was not *when* I wanted to die. If I died, Mom would be out on the streets. Not to mention I'd abandoned her just like Dad had left us. I had to at least try to save our farm. I couldn't give up yet, not before I'd even started.

I looked out again. Not only were the flames getting closer, but a bunch of people were running toward us. People waving swords and shovels that looked like they'd kill anyone who got in their way, which we, being inside this horse, definitely were.

"Okay, I'll make you a deal, Dory. If you get out of this horse then …" My voice drifted off. What did I possibly have to offer Dory? Potatoes and a couple strips of bacon from our farm?

"Then what?"

I bit my lip. "What do you want? Name it, and I'll do it. Just hurry."

Dory didn't hesitate. "I want you to teach me to read and write."

Everyone knew that teaching a slave to read and write was illegal. The penalty was something horrible like getting your hands chopped off or your fingernails pulled out or an equally torturous punishment like that. But I figured that was the least of my worries. I could start teaching Dory, and when he saw how hard it was, he'd give up and no one would ever find out.

"Done," I said. "Just get off your butt and come on."

"You promise, Homer?" he said.

"I promise. Now move."

That's all it took. Okay, it also took me holding Dory out over the edge of the opening as far as I could so his drop would be small. Then, of course, I had to jump after him. But the on-coming hoards and fire hurried me. I landed hard on one of the horse's giant wooden wheels, but I got up super-fast and ig-nored the shooting pain that went up my back. Then, I grabbed Dory's hand, and we bolted away from the crowd.

We had to wind around tons of people screaming and

buildings burning, and I was certain at least eight different times that we'd come to our end. The battle raged the entire night. We hid behind barrels and buildings and even tucked away in a sewer for part of it. But then the sun came up from over the horizon, and the gates loomed open before us, and we dashed through, out of the city and toward the beach.

"To the boats!" Odysseus shouted. He stood near a dozen black ships with bright blue sails all anchored out in the water. "The battle is won! We're going home!"

Home sounded great to me. I had totally gotten everything I needed to fill the scroll. I pictured myself relaxing on the boat, writing out all the details from the battle while Odysseus took us back to Ionia. This would totally keep me in school. Except then Dory saw the cat.

"Homer, look!" Dory said, elbowing me hard.

It was stuck on top of the city walls. Fire came at it from both sides. It was too far away to hear, but it kept opening its mouth like it was crying. And even though I wasn't much of a cat person despite the fact that we had like a thousand of them running around the farm, a twang of sadness washed over me. Like it was this one tiny creature in this huge battle without a chance.

Dory took a step toward it but then stepped back and bit his lip.

"What do you think you're doing?" I said.

"Someone should save it," Dory said. But he didn't move forward.

I was about to disagree when the cat meowed and cried again, and the sound drifted over the horrendous battle, a pitiful wailing that wormed its way inside me, almost like we were supposed to hear it. And I knew that even if this cat was completely unimportant, Dory was right. Someone had to save it. But after the whole jumping out of the horse incident, that someone wasn't going to be Dory. He'd never get past how high the city walls were.

"I'll get it," I said, regretting the words the second they left my lips.

Dory gritted his teeth and glanced back at the boats. "Odysseus is about it leave."

"I know. I'll be right back. I have to save the cat."

I didn't stick around to wait for him to say anything else. Instead I took off, back for the burning walls of Troy. Once I got to the bottom of the wall, I scoured the area, looking for anything that would help me get up to the top. From here the cat's howls were deafening over the crackling fire.

Off to my left were a few barrels, but they were too close to the flames. The right was no better. Some crates had been smashed to pieces. I didn't need much. If I could just get something to raise me up about five feet, I could grab the ledge.

"Here, foot up," Dory said.

I turned to find him behind me, clasping his hands. I didn't waste time. I stepped into his handhold and hefted myself up. But it wasn't enough. I was about six inches too short.

"Sorry about this," I said, and I stepped on Dory's head.

32

He let out a bunch of words I'm not going to repeat, because I didn't want to risk Elder Pachis saying my story wasn't age appropriate. Not that I had any idea who, if anyone, would ever read my story besides him.

But the extra height was enough. My fingers grasped the ledge. I pulled myself up, even with my puny muscles. And then I balanced on the ledge.

"Here, Kitty." I held my hands out, praying to the gods that I didn't fall and break my neck.

The cat wasted no time. It launched at me and landed on my head, digging its claws into my scalp. Payback for me stepping on Dory's head, no doubt. But that was okay. I had the thing.

I lowered myself until I hung from the ledge, and then I dropped.

From out of nowhere, a little girl ran up and grabbed the cat off my head. She looked like she was about three years old and wore a tattered green dress and had dark hair and long eyelashes that made her green eyes look super huge.

"You saved Grumpy," she said, and she hugged the cat so hard to her chest that I worried she was going to crush him.

"Yeah, I did," I said. I reached out to rub the top of her head, but she jumped back like she thought I was going to poison her with my touch. And here I was the one who'd just saved her cat. Also what kind of name was Grumpy for a cat, anyway?

But then Dory reached out and scratched the cat between the ears, and neither the little girl nor the cat seemed to mind.

"I always wanted a cat," Dory said.

"We need to go now," I said, yanking on Dory's arm.

The lifeboat was already away from the beach. The little girl's eyes grew wide at the sight of the ships, and then she whipped around so fast, her tangled dark hair flew around in a giant circle, showing off a huge smudge of dirt on the back of her neck. Or maybe a tattoo, because it almost seemed to have a pattern to it. Then she ran away.

We dug our feet into the sand and ran for the boats. All the hairy, smelly guys were already aboard, too, holding weapons and treasures from the burning city of Troy. They grinned like … like … I had no idea.

"What's a good comparison for the way they're grinning?" I asked Dory.

"You mean like a simile?" Dory said.

"Sure." Whatever that was.

Dory thought for a second, then said, "They grinned like they just won the war!"

"Right. Like victory. That's good. I'll use it. Elder Pachis is sure to like that." I was becoming a master storyteller, and I hadn't even put a word down on the scroll yet.

The water pushed against us as we waded through it, but it was no match for our determination. I was going to get on this boat and go home. When we finally got within reach, some of the guys hauled us onboard.

I found a corner to sit out of the way, filled my pen with ink, and started writing. This was the epic story that would save our farm, and I was not going to forget a second of it. I had to fill the entire scroll.

Odysseus shouted a couple commands, and everyone jumped into motion, running around, pulling on ropes, turning wheels. Then the boats started really moving, leaving the burning city of Troy far behind.

"You ready to teach me?" Dory said.

I shook my head, not slowing down. I had to get the story out.

"I'll teach you once we get back to Ionia," I said. There would be plenty of time to teach Dory to read and write, unless of course I was cast out onto the streets. Then my life would be basically over. Right now, I had to get this story down.

"No way, Homer," Dory said. "You promised."

"And I'll keep my promise," I said. "As soon as we get back to Ionia."

"Ionia?" some burly guy that looked like he bench-pressed Doric columns for fun said. His skin was dark, like the color of ebony. Actually, come to think of it, all of the guys and Odysseus himself had dark skin. I'd seen skin that color a few times when we traveled to some of the coastal cities, but never in Ionia.

Dory kind of shrugged like maybe he was embarrassed by the fact that we were from such a backward place. Coastal cities were a lot more fun, if rumors could be believed. "It's where we're from."

"Yeah, we're going back there," I said.

The burly guy shook his head. "We're not going to Ionia. We sail to Ithaca."

Ithaca! That was on the other side of the universe. Or maybe at least the other side of the sea. I don't know. I'd fallen asleep during Geography. Still, that wasn't going to work at all.

"Wait. Why Ithaca?" Dory said.

The guy looked at us like we'd lost our brains in the battle of Troy. "Because Odysseus is king of Ithaca."

The big smelly guy was a king? No way. I tried to picture him with a crown on, getting his feet rubbed by servants, but I just couldn't. All he'd done so far was give one sentence commands and burn down an entire city. He also struck me as loud and impulsive and not so smart.

I opened my mouth to ask if maybe I'd heard wrong, but right then, Odysseus, the king, sauntered up. The bulky guy bowed his head and stepped back.

"Excuse me, Odysseus?" I said. Was I supposed to call him King Odysseus? He wasn't my king.

"What is it?" he asked, hardly casting a glance at me or Dory.

"We need to get to Ionia," I said.

He shook his hairy head. "Not going to happen. We sail straight for Ithaca. And nothing is going to get in our way."

As You Set Out
For Ithaca

Turned out that everyone on the boat needed a job.

"No free rides," Eurylochus said in his whiny voice when he discovered Dory and I stowed away behind some barrels.

"It's Dory and me," Dory said. "Not Dory and I."

I smudged the words on the scroll and changed it. Dory may not know much when it came to reading and writing, but he had this grammar thing down. I'd asked him about the Dactylic Hexameter part of it, but sadly he had no clue.

"I have a job," I said, holding up the scroll.

Eurylochus narrowed his eyes like he thought the scroll was some sort of weapon. "What're you gonna do with that?" As he spoke, he stroked his beard. He'd trimmed it since the battle with Troy was over. His dark skin glistened, but not with sweat, like he'd put in a hard day's work. More like he'd smoothed oil on himself. And his nails had been cleaned and filed and buffed so much the sun reflected off them.

"I'm recording the story," I said. "It's really important. It will make the Trojan Horse famous." That's what I'd called it in the story. The Trojan Horse. I thought it was pretty catchy. It was also a pretty clever idea. Odysseus himself had come up with it, according to what we'd overheard from the guys. Maybe he was smarter than he seemed at first glance.

"Have you approved that with King Odysseus?" Eurylochus asked, still stroking his beard. It formed a perfect point at the bottom of his chin.

"Sure," I said, even though I hadn't. Not really.

Okay, not at all. But since Odysseus was the main character of the Trojan Horse story, I was sure he'd be fine with it.

Eurylochus either believed me or didn't want to question me anymore in case it might make him look stupid.

"What'd'bout you?" he said to Dory. "What're you good for?"

Dory shrugged. "I can cook."

Eurylochus stoked his beard again since it had been over two seconds since the last time he did it. "Well, our last cook did get thrown overboard and eaten by a giant octopus."

"He got thrown overboard?" I said.

Eurylochus nodded. "Nobody liked his cooking."

I shuddered. But Dory just smiled.

And that's how Dory got his job.

Ψ

"SO WE GO TO ITHACA AND THEN FIND A WAY TO Ionia from there," I said to Dory. He was in the galley—that's what some guy with an eyepatch told us the kitchen on a boat is called—covered in grain, mushing a bunch of dough he assured me would make bread. I hoped someone in Ithaca knew about Dactylic Hexameter.

"We could just stay in Ithaca," Dory said.

"Are you kidding? No way. Why would we do that?"

"I don't know," Dory said. "What if we can't find a way to get back to Ionia from there?"

"We'll find a way," I said. There was no way I was staying in Ithaca. I was going to get back to Ionia, finish school, and become a soldier. My future was mapped out.

"If you say so."

"I do say so," I said. Dory acted like he didn't want to get back. But that wasn't even an option for me. Even though she didn't know it, Mom was counting on me. I was not going to let her down.

I grabbed the hourglass from the rope around my neck and checked the sand level. It wasn't even a fourth empty. Not even an eighth. But the sand still fell from the top to the bottom. Which was weird. Two full days had gone by. I tapped it, just to check. The sand slipped through, grain by grain.

"How long will it take to get to Ithaca?" Dory asked. "These guys eat so much food. It's not going to last that much longer."

The galley was connected to a storeroom, more empty than not, which was great because that's where Dory and I slept. One benefit of being the cook. Otherwise we'd be stuck below deck in hammocks listening to fifty snoring guys.

"Less than a week, Odysseus says. I asked him," I said. At less than a week, I'd still have time to get back to Ionia. Sure, there was no time to waste, but it would all work out.

Dory looked to the shelves in the storeroom and seemed to do some sort of mental math. "A week," he said. "We should be able to stretch it that far."

"Stretch what that far?" Odysseus said, sauntering in. Since the last time I'd seen him, he'd cleaned up quite a bit. He wore a fresh yellow tunic, and his dark hair and beard had been trimmed and washed to the point where I hoped he'd gotten rid of all the lice. Lice was not anything I wanted to experience again. I'd had it once and had to endure hours of Mom picking through my hair, removing it.

"Not too much backstory," Dory said. He'd been saying this a lot. I guess talking about having lice when I was five years old might be considered backstory. So I scratched out a couple of the other sentences. I did leave in the part about how his royal pain-in-my-butt, Demetrios, had lice, too. He was probably the one who gave it to me.

"Stretch our food for the next week," Dory said. "I should be able to make it last that long. But it would be helpful if you asked the guys not to eat so much."

"Nonsense," Odysseus said. "My men have spent the last ten years fighting a war. They will eat however much they want."

Dory grimaced. This was a perfect example of Odysseus not being all that smart.

I kept my mouth shut. Not Dory.

"Fine," Dory said, putting his grain-covered hands on his hips in a totally non-dude-like way. "We're going to run out."

Odysseus closed his mouth and seemed to ponder this deep statement. He placed a finger to his lips. I noticed he did this when he thought a big decision was coming. Finally, he snapped his fingers.

"I have a solution," he said. "We'll stop in Ismaros."

"Stop!" I said. "I thought we were heading straight to Ithaca." Stopping was not part of the plan. I had to get home and get back to school.

Odysseus waved my comment away like it was of no concern. "Don't worry, little Bard. It'll only be a day out of our way. We'll stop at the port, find provisions, and then be on our way."

Little Bard. What kind of nickname was that? Like I was some kind of pet he was keeping around. But I didn't complain because I'd rather be writing the story than cleaning up after his guys, and I didn't see myself as qualified for much else on the ship. I may want to be a soldier when I was older, but I wasn't ready yet.

"Only a day?" I said.

Odysseus' face filled with his kingly confidence. The kind that said "this is my decision and you better not question it."

"Only a day," he said.

So, we set sail for Ismaros.

Okay, side note here. I have to mention that Odysseus was wrong. I'd noticed this was a recurring habit of his. Instead of the promised one day, it took us nearly four days to reach Ismaros. I panicked the first day and the second, but then I noticed that the hourglass still moved in slow motion, as if maybe in this adventure Hermes had sent us on, time moved differently. That had to be within the power of the gods. I mean, there was even a god of time, Kronos. Maybe he and Hermes were in this thing together. Anyway, I tried not to panic even though I was about to go down there and row the boats myself.

Because. That. Was. The. Problem.

The men didn't want to row the boats. All they wanted to do was party. And even Odysseus, with his kingly commands, had a hard time controlling them. It was only when Dory served cold stone soup for dinner that they finally got the idea. If they didn't start rowing, they'd die of starvation.

"Where'd you get the idea for stone soup?" I asked as I drew a little picture of the port of Ismaros. I'd never been so happy to see land. I was going to get off this boat and get some fresh air, even if it was only for a few hours.

Dory shrugged. "Back in Ionia. Demetrios' dad is actually the one who told me about it."

"He told you about soup made with stones? For him to eat?"

"No. Of course not. To feed the peasants who beg at his door every day."

"He feeds the peasants stone soup?" As if I didn't already think Demetrios and his family were worthless. I had no clue how they'd managed to come to power. It seemed like King Telamon was losing power, at least within Ionia. Something about the royal line dying off.

"Pretty bad, right?" Dory said. "And that's only minimal compared to some of the other stuff they do."

"I wish you didn't have to go back to them," I said. Sure, Mom and I did plenty of hard labor, but we owned the farm. Dory was a slave which meant that he'd never be able to own anything. He'd always be owned. The only way for slaves to be freed was if their masters granted it, and I couldn't imagine Demetrios or his family doing anything nice without some ulterior motive.

"Whatever," Dory said, but he turned away. I didn't push it, but I reaffirmed my promise to him. I may not be legally allowed to teach him to read and write, but I was going to, no matter what the risk. Maybe then, once we got back, he'd have some kind of chance at something besides a life of slavery.

It all Starts with One Bad Choice

Odysseus ordered all the boats but his to anchor offshore. Since there were twelve boats, they wouldn't all fit at the dock. Luckily for us, this meant we didn't have to wade through the water which was dull and gray like the sky. I guess it's good when you're the king.

"What's our budget?" Dory asked Odysseus as we came up onto the deck.

"Budget?" Odysseus looked perplexed.

"Yeah, for our provisions," Dory said. "We need food, water. Alcohol will be pricier, so we may want to not get so much of that. We'll also be needing first aid supplies. Bandages. Salves."

"Bandages? Salves?" Odysseus scratched his head. "For what?"

"In case anyone gets hurt."

Odysseus let out a bellowing laugh. "In case anyone gets hurt! That's a good one!"

I guess Odysseus didn't think anyone was going to get hurt. "Okay, then just the other provisions," Dory said. "What's the budget?" He put his hand out for some gold coins.

Odysseus looked at the hand with curiosity but didn't offer anything to put it in. "We ask for provisions," Odysseus said. "We don't pay for them. These men just fought in a ten-year long war to defend Greece. We will not be paying for anything that is rightfully ours."

Dory gritted his teeth like he was trying really hard to keep from saying something completely disrespectful to Odysseus. "So, you're not planning on paying for anything?"

"Of course not."

"You're sure?" Dory said.

"Absolutely," Odysseus said.

This visit was going to be a disaster.

Since Dory wasn't about to go steal food from the locals—we'd leave that up to the guys—he and I set out into the city. I needed to track down someone who knew something about storytelling.

"Not storytelling," Dory said. "You're doing fine with that part. Just the format of the story."

Right. I needed to find someone who understood Dactylic Hexameter, because that someone was not me.

We went door to door in the rainy weather, talking to the Cicones—that's what the people who lived in the city were called. They didn't speak quite the same language as we did, but it was enough to get some basic messages passed back and forth. Writing. Stories. Some old dude with a ton of missing teeth finally pointed to the hills on the outskirts of the city and told us to find Old Lady Tessa. Just as we were setting out on the path out of the city, someone grabbed us from behind.

"Where do you two think you're going?"

We turned to find one of Odysseus' men—the guy with the eyepatch—holding us at the shoulders. In addition to the bright red eyepatch, he also had a bum leg that made him limp when he walked. And his hair was done up in at least a hundred tiny little braids, each with a seashell at the end like personal, portable wind chimes.

"We need to talk to an old lady," I said.

"And you're going alone?" he said.

I tossed up my hands. "Sure. Why wouldn't we be?" We were twelve. Almost teenagers. It's not like we needed to have our mommies with us at all given times. Plus, how dangerous could some old hag be?

"I'll come along," he said.

"Okay, sure," I said. It didn't much matter to me. Also, he did have a sword which would be handy if we ran into a wild boar or something.

We set out walking again, and though the guy limped on his leg, it didn't slow him down too much.

"My name's Polites," the guy said. He said it like Po-Light-Us.

Dory and I had been trying to settle on a nickname for him

for the last couple days. I'd suggested Patch but Dory told me that wasn't politically correct.

"Polites," I said, happy to know his real name. "Bet you have good manners."

"Never heard that one before," Polites said, and he made some weird funny laugh that kind of bounced around in the back of his throat. I hoped it meant he thought my joke was at least kind of funny.

"Why aren't you helping get food?" Dory asked. "Don't they need you to haul stuff onto the boats?"

"Tomorrow they will," Polites said. "Today all they'll do is drink mead."

I'd found out a year ago that mead was this completely gross old-person drink that made me puke for three hours straight the one time I'd tried a sip. I completely don't recommend it unless you want to suffer the same fate as me.

"It's pretty cool that these people are going to share so much with us," I said.

"Yeah, sharing," Polites said, and he did that weird funny laugh thing again. "So where are we going, anyway?"

"Old Lady Tessa's," I said. "She lives in a shack up in the hills."

"The guy who told us about her said she was some kind of witch," Dory added.

Polites scratched behind his eyepatch and then readjusted it. "And why are we going to see some witch?"

Oy. I hoped she wasn't a witch. I'd never met a witch first-hand, but Elder Pachis told us in school that witches would put a curse on you so fast, you'd be begging to end your own existence. Living an entire life never meeting a real witch would be fine with me.

"She knows Dactylic Hexameter," I said. "Or at least that's what some old geezer down in town told us."

"What's Dactylic Hexameter?" Polites asked.

"That's what we need to find out," I said.

The three of us left the city and started up into the hills. Since they were all rocky and barren, nobody else lived there, so it didn't take long at all to find the rundown little shack. And I hated to admit it, but with all the wind chimes hanging from the rafters and the glass jars on the windowsills, it did look like the kind of place a witch would live.

"Gods help me," I said. "The only reason I'm doing this is for Mom." Bringing home the story wasn't going to be good enough. With the battle at Troy, I'd already gotten more than enough adventure to fill the scroll. Now I just needed to make it right.

I knocked on the door, afraid it would disintegrate under the force of my fist. The witch would put a curse on me for sure if that happened.

The door opened instantly, as if whoever was on the other side was standing there waiting for us. A really cute lady, who was probably younger than Mom, stood there. She had big green eyes and dark, dark hair with skin to match.

"I saw you coming," she said.

I opened my mouth to speak, but words wouldn't come

out. Polites seemed to be having the same problem.

But Dory wasn't having any issues. "We're looking for Old Lady Tessa. She's supposed to be some old hag who lives up around here."

The woman grinned and winked at us. "You found her."

It took me a second to realize that she was talking about herself.

"You?" I said.

"Me!"

"But you're not old."

"And neither are you," Old Lady Tessa said, reaching out to pinch my cheek. I stepped back out of her reach. "What are you, ten?"

I stood up a little taller. "Twelve. Almost thirteen." Actually, I wouldn't be thirteen for another six months.

"I'm twenty-nine," Polites said, smoothing his braids and making sure his red eyepatch was lying flat.

Oh gods. If he started flirting with her, I was going to throw up.

"This old guy down in the village told us you could help us," Dory said.

Old Lady Tessa opened the door wider, inviting us in. And though the outside of the shack looked like it would blow down if the breeze picked up, the inside was spotless.

"Sure, I'll help," she said.

Against every sane bone in my body, I stepped inside. I had to make my story right.

Old Lady Tessa closed the door behind us. I realized that we were trapped. There was no easy way out now.

"Are you a witch?" I asked. If we'd allowed ourselves to be locked in the house of a witch, we'd deserve our fate. She was probably about to throw us in the oven and bake us into cookies.

Polites elbowed me, hard.

Old Lady Tessa just laughed. "I'm not a witch. Well, not really too much of a witch."

I wasn't sure if that was supposed to be comforting or not.

"Now what do you need help with?" she asked.

"Dactylic Hexameter," I said.

Old Lady Tessa—well, she wasn't really an old lady, so just Tessa—clasped her hands together. "Oh, I love Dactylic Hexameter. Second only to Iambic Hexameter. King of the meters. I could speak it all day. Let's see …

"There once was a meter I knew.
I spoke it when I put on my shoe.
I knew all the beats.
They sounded so sweet.
I also made a mean beef stew."

Relief flooded through me. We'd definitely come to the right spot.

"Beef stew?" Dory said, narrowing his eyes at Tessa. "What does that have to do with Dactylic Hexameter?"

"Yeah, rhyme isn't my strongest skill," Tessa said. "It's trickier

50

than people think. Everyone thinks writing little rhyming poems is simple, but it takes practice. Lots and lots of practice."

"It would be my epic debut," I suggested, thinking about how
amazing my story was going to be. And *debut* totally rhymed
with *shoe.*

"Good," Tessa said. "I like that. *Epic debut.*"

"So is that Dactylic Hexameter?" I asked. I grabbed my
scroll and pen and prepared to take a few notes in the margin. If
that's all there was to Dactylic Hexameter, I'd get it no problem.

"Oh, no," Tessa said. "That's a silly little limerick. Dactylic
Hexameter is way harder than that. It's the heroic hexameter.
The meter of epic. Only the greatest of stories deserve to be
told in Dactylic Hexameter."

No pressure or anything. I was so not the right person for
this job. But Old Man Pachis had said I needed an epic story.
And sure, maybe this whole Dactylic Hexameter thing was one
more stupid test of his, but if it made the difference between
keeping me in school or having us cast out onto the streets, I
was going to give it my best.

"Teach me," I said.

Polites eyed me. "Manners," he said.

"I mean, teach me, please?"

Tessa launched into some lengthy explanation about long
syllables and short syllables and trochees and anceps and
spondees and caesura and diphthongs. And after the first five
minutes, it all started sounding the same to me. But I pushed
past the normal sleepiness that would have taken over were I

back in the barn schoolhouse, and I tried. I really focused. And pretty soon, words started coming together in my mind. They took shape and made structure, and I could see the syllables like real elements floating in the air, waiting for me to grasp and manipulate.

"Time for a break," Polites said, refilling his mead jug.

"A break!" I said. "But I'm just starting to get the hang of it."

"We've been at it for hours," Polites said.

"No way," I said. "It's only been, like …" I checked my dad's hourglass, but the sand was still barely moving. I couldn't count on it for real time. And the only sundial I'd seen was back in town.

"It's been four hours," Tessa said. "Polites is right. You're doing great. Time to break."

Tessa and Dory made us dinner. Polites and I went outside to wait because they said we were just getting in the way. And though I couldn't hear anything they were talking about, there sure was a lot of giggling coming from inside the shack. Hopefully Dory would tell me what was so funny, because Polites and I just sat there, not talking, looking out at the boats on the water. There were no sign of Odysseus and the guys leaving, and seeing as how it was almost night, I figured the earliest we'd leave would be the morning.

An hour went by with neither of us saying a word, but finally Polites said, "The villagers are running away."

He was right. The Cicones had taken off from Ismaros, heading north.

"I wonder / what the / reason for / them flee / ing so haste / ily is," I answered in perfect Dactylic Hexameter. Or at least as perfect as I'd gotten it down so far. I wasn't keen on splitting my words across the feet, but I'd only just learned today. I would get better.

Polites smacked me upside the head. Not in a mean way. More in a fun way. The kind of way Dad used to do when we'd sit outside and watch the stars and I'd start making up funny names for the constellations. It made this really weird lump form in my throat, so I kept the next line of Dactylic Hexameter to myself. But I loved this hexameter stuff. I planned to speak this way all the time.

"Side note, Homer. That's a horrible idea. I'm not going to be your friend if you talk like that," Dory said later, as I was writing down the whole incident.

I left the sentence anyway.

"I'll tell you the reason they're running away," Tessa said, opening the shack door. Whatever scents came from inside made my stomach growl. Maybe it was beef stew. I could not wait to eat.

"What?" I asked.

"Your men," Tessa said. "They've sacked the village."

Urg. I wanted to choke Odysseus.

"I knew it was a bad idea to expect the Cicones to just give us stuff," Dory said.

"They'll be back in the morning," Tessa said. "With reinforcements."

"And that's when we'll be going," Polites said. And then he kind of smiled at Tessa, and she smiled back, and I wanted to roll my eyes because he was completely flirting with her.

So, we ate our dinner and then went to bed. Dory and I slept outside so we could keep watch—or at least hear if there was any kind of commotion. There was commotion, but not coming from the beach. Still, I managed to drift off to sleep.

I woke to Polites limp-running from the shack.

"We need to go now!" he said.

Dory and I jumped to our feet.

"Safe and swift travels," Tessa said from the doorway.

At this, Polites stopped and turned back and bowed deeply to Tessa and then kissed her on the hand. "I hope our paths cross again."

"Oh, they will," she said, like she could see the future or something.

Already some sort of fight had broken out on the beach. The sound of steel hitting steel echoed through the air.

"Thank you!" I said, remembering my manners.

Tessa grabbed my hand. "Homer?"

"What?" I asked, watching Polites and Dory clamber down the path.

"I'm not a witch," she said.

"Thank the gods," I said. Now that I'd learned Dactylic Hexameter, I didn't want her to turn me into a toad.

"But I can see the future," she said.

I knew it!

"Do I become a soldier? Do I save the farm?" I asked. "Is the story good enough?"

She shook her head. "I don't know, Homer. But I do know this. The mark is the secret."

"What mark?" I asked. I had no clue what she was talking about.

"The mark is the secret," she said again. "That's all I know. It's important."

The mark is the secret. I doubted I'd ever know what it meant, but it didn't really matter.

"Thank you, I guess," I said.

She gave my hand a squeeze and let go. "Watch out for Dory."

"I will," I said, and then I ran, catching up with Polites and Dory. With his bum leg, Polites couldn't move all that fast, but we hurried as best we could.

When we finally came down out of the hills and got back to Ismaros, the peacefulness of the night before had vanished. The Cicones had come back early this morning and fought with a vengeance. Some of Odysseus' guys fought them, some grabbed as much food and drink as they could. I figured we'd find food elsewhere.

"We need to get to the boats," I said, but the city was a mess. Dory and I were small enough that we were able to cut and curve around most of the action. The fighting thickened once we got to the beach. Polites ran to Odysseus' side and joined in, battling five skinny dudes that had no reason picking a fight in the first place. And to Odysseus' credit, he didn't kill them. He only fought them off until most of his men had cleared the town.

"To the boats!" he called.

The guys didn't need to be told twice. They ran, dropping melons and mead bottles on the way. Dory and I ran, too. Since our ship was anchored to the dock, we jumped aboard. And in the quickest two minutes of my life, the ship pushed off and headed away from Ismaros.

"Well, that went nicely," Eurylochus said, patting Odysseus on the back.

"Are you insane, man?" Odysseus said. "That went horribly. We fought innocent people. We lost men." His yellow shirt was ripped nearly in half, showing off his enormous muscles. He also sported cuts on his arms and chest, just like a lot of the guys.

"Our provisions are full," Eurylochus said, as if that justified everything.

"We don't fight with villagers," Odysseus said. "It will anger the gods." He put his head in his hands like he couldn't believe the awful turn of events.

I wanted to pipe in and mention how Odysseus was the one who'd suggested taking food from the villagers in the first place, but I kept my mouth shut. Still, in my head, I constructed a brilliant retort in Dactylic Hexameter.

"Does it seem exceptionally windy?" Polites said. He still had the same perma-grin on his face that had been there since we met Tessa.

Odysseus licked his finger and held it up into the air. The bright blue sails billowed in the wind. "Exceptionally. And ..."

"And what?" I said.

The concern grew on his face with every passing second. The ships moved with a vengeance through the water.

"And it's blowing the wrong way."

FLOWER CHILDREN

THIS WAS WHERE THE GODS GOT MAD. I MAY HAVE been just a farm boy, but I knew that the wind didn't blow for nine days straight in the complete opposite direction of Ithaca just by coincidence. Odysseus and his guys had really ticked the gods off. Their stupid, selfish pilfering was going to do us all in.

I wasn't sure which god Odysseus had upset. He complained about a bunch of them. Except for Athena. The way he talked about Athena made me think he wasn't thinking about his wife, Penelope, at home all that much. Not that it was any of my business.

"Then why are you writing it down?" Dory asked. Since we'd had a whole bunch of free time in the last nine days, I'd started teaching him. He could sing the entire alphabet song and recognized all the letters. We found the old gold paint they'd used to paint the Trojan Horse and had starting writing letters on the walls of the storage room. Dory's writing wasn't bad though he kept getting phi and psi confused.

"I just wrote that Athena is Odysseus' favorite god," I said. "I left out the part about his wife."

"That's good," Dory said. "Women don't want to read stuff like that about their husbands."

I wasn't sure how Dory knew this, but I was too busy counting syllables to ask.

The afternoon of the ninth day, Polites, who was perched up in the crow's nest because even though he only had one eye, he could see farther than anyone else on the ship, hollered, "Land!"

The guys erupted with cheering. This was because in addition to having no control of the boat for nine days thanks to the wind, we also hadn't seen any land. It didn't take a genius to guess that we were going to dock.

"Gods above, let this not be another Ismaros," Dory said. "And also, let's hope they have some fruit. If we go much longer without it, people's teeth are going to start to fall out."

Lots of the guys already had missing teeth, a testament to the number of fights they'd been in. It made my dreams of being a soldier seem not quite so glamorous. I hoped for their sake we found fruit, too. They couldn't stand to lose any more.

The boats pulled into the port, and like before, our boat was the only one to actually dock. For the others, the guys had to row ashore in life boats.

Odysseus jumped to the dock first. "We only take what we're offered," he said, like he was talking to small children.

"What if they have mead?" this one stupid-looking guy who I was pretty sure was drunk most of the time said. Dory and I had started calling him Rum.

"Only if it's offered," Odysseus said.

"Or cake," a chubby guy we called Cupcake said. "I love cake."

"Only if it's offered," Odysseus said.

It continued on this way. I would have used up the entire scroll if I'd written down all their comments. Suffice it to say, they covered every possible edible. And no sooner did Odysseus turn his back, they all ran off, straight for the city, Rum and Cupcake leading the way.

"We should go, too," Dory said. "Check for fruit."

"Do we have anything to trade?" I asked.

Dory put his hands together into a big zero. "Nope. But I'm hoping they'll take pity on us since we're kids."

Polites limped over to join us. "I'll come with you two. Keep you out of trouble."

We hadn't gotten into any trouble before, but I didn't mind Polites. He got along with most everyone, even that slimy weasel Eurylochus, which was the equivalent to getting along with a rodent.

"Moldy bread," Dory said. "That's what Eurylochus reminds me of."

"Not a rodent?" I asked. Here I'd thought the whole simile

thing was pretty clever.

"Some people think rodents are cute," Dory said.

I wasn't sure what people he was talking about. Maybe Demetrios back in Ionia?

"Nobody thinks moldy bread is cute," Dory said.

That was true.

"Are you coming?" Polites asked Odysseus.

Odysseus narrowed his eyes and studied the city ahead. It was hard to see much of anything from here except the men running toward it. "Not yet. But report back to me if you see anything suspicious. I have a funny feeling about this place."

That didn't fill me with confidence. Still, we'd been on the boat for nine days. My stomach and legs needed a break.

Polites, Dory, and I headed toward the city. It was weird, because even though Rum and Cupcake hadn't left all that long before us, they were already out of sight. Of course, they were running, and we weren't.

"How'd you hurt your leg?" I asked Polites. "And how'd you lose your eye?"

"Right to the point, I see," he said.

I shrugged and shifted the pen in my fingers. "I'm a story-teller. What can I say? I'm out to get information."

In addition to the entire Trojan Horse thing, I'd added every detail from Ismaros. Elder Pachis was going to pee his pants with excitement when he saw what an epic story I'd written. I figured anything from this point on was just icing on the cake.

"Will you write about it?" Polites asked.

"Are you a hero? Did you do something heroic?" I asked. After all, my story was supposed to be totally heroic.

"Maybe," Polites said.

"Well then, maybe I'll write about it," I said.

At that Polites laughed. "I got it defending Odysseus."

"Against who?" I said.

"Against whom," Dory corrected. "Against is a preposition."

I wasn't sure what a preposition was, but I added the extra letter and kept writing.

"Against Ajax," Polites said.

"Ajax?" Dory said. "I've heard rumors about that guy. But wasn't he a Greek?"

"Sure," Polites said. "But he and Odysseus … They had this disagreement going on for years. It had all sorts of things to do with racing and Athena and glory and victory. And this one time, about halfway through the battle, things got a little heated. They started fighting, out on the beach, in the middle of everyone. Ajax cursed the name of Athena. Odysseus was not going to stand for that. But you know Odysseus. He's smart, but he's a little impulsive. He'd been drinking all night and had no right to get into a fight."

"So, you stepped in and saved him?" I asked.

"Yeah," Polites said. "I stepped in and saved him. Lost my eye. Hurt my leg. But, you know, these things happen."

"So, you are kind of a hero," I said.

"I wouldn't be upset if you wrote that," Polites said, and then he winked at me. Or at least I think he did. With an eyepatch, it's hard to tell when someone's winking.

"You guys see that?" Dory had stopped walking and pointed ahead.

We were over halfway across the beach, but someone must've seen us because there were a few people headed our way.

Polites' hand immediately went to his sword. I grabbed my pen. For my purposes, the pen was definitely mightier that the sword.

"They look friendly," Dory said, squinting ahead.

"Looks can be deceiving," Polites said.

But I had to agree with Dory. The three people heading our way looked like they were dressed to go out visiting temples in their finest clothes. As they got closer, I could see that their hair was brushed until it shone, their teeth sparkled in the sunlight, but best of all, they carried trays loaded with flowers and fresh fruit.

It took everything in me not to run directly toward them and start shoving the fruit into my mouth like a starving sailor. No offense to the guys on the boat. Let's just say that they didn't have the best of manners.

"Fruit!" Dory said, and he took off running.

So much for manners.

I ran after him, and Polites hurried as best he could. And when I reached the people and saw how plump and juicy the fruit was, I was ready to trade away the scroll and my pen just for one small bite.

"Would you like refreshments, young travelers?" one of the

three people said. It was a guy in a white toga with gold twine wrapped around it.

"You don't mind?" I almost drooled at the sight of it.

"Of course not," another of the people said. It was another guy, maybe a couple years older than the first, in a green toga the same color as Dory's shirt.

"We want to share," the third said, this one a girl. She was probably only about twenty and wore a purple toga.

"Well, in that case," Dory said, and he grabbed a fresh peach with a huge flower attached to the top of it from the platter. Polites and I were right behind him, and when the juice from the fruit hit my lips, I was sure I'd died and gone to the Elysian Fields.

"Thank you so much," I said, after about five bites. Mom would be horribly upset with me if I forgot to thank them, even if my excuse was that I was starving to death.

"It's our pleasure," the first guy said.

And they all smiled, brilliant smiles. And their eyes shone. It was kinda weird because even though their skin colors were varied, they all had the same bright blue eyes, like the ocean, where I could almost see right through them.

"Would you like some more?" the girl asked.

We all did, so we followed them back in the direction they'd come from. When we reached the town, all of the guys from the boats had already made themselves comfortable. Eurylochus was stretched out on a lounge chair with an entire plate of fruit and flowers on a table next to him. Rum and Cupcake and three other guys sat around a table, sharing trays, passing them around and trying all the different varieties that were offered.

With twelve ships and fifty guys per ship, that was a lot of sailors to feed, but the people—I didn't know what they called themselves—didn't seem to care. Speaking of which, that seemed like a pretty big oversight on my part. I needed details.

"What are your people called?" I asked as we followed the two guys and the girl to a table with a giant umbrella overhead. It blocked out the hot sun perfectly, and mist floated through the air down onto our heads.

"We're just the Flower Children," the girl said, and she sat down, so we all did. And even though I'd just eaten four huge pieces of fruit, my stomach grumbled.

The table was decorated with bright flowers that were so plump and full of life that they almost looked like they could be eaten, too. Not that I was going to eat flowers.

"Are flowers poisonous?" I asked Dory.

Dory shook his head. But it almost seemed kind of slowed down, and he smiled really slightly, almost like the sly grin I'd seen girls at school give. Well, they never gave those grins to me. More Demetrios, since he was rich and his dad was the mayor.

"Some flowers are poisonous," Dory said. "But not these." And he picked one up and ate it in a single bite.

I turned to look, but somewhere along the way to the table, we'd lost Polites. It was just me and Dory and the flower children who'd led us here.

"I should write this down," I said, unrolling my scroll.

65

"What are you writing?" she asked, but she didn't look down at the scroll or anything, so I got the distinct feeling that she didn't really care.

"Just a story," I said.

"Can I read it?" she asked.

"I guess," I said, pushing the scroll her way.

"Here, have a flower while I read." She handed me two of the plump flowers from the table, and since Dory hadn't died yet from eating them, I figured they'd be okay. So, I popped one in my mouth.

I'd never had candy, but I imagine that once candy got invented, it would taste like these flowers. Because they melted in my mouth and soothed my stomach and made my head go all happy. And all I could think was that I wanted more. So, I popped another in my mouth, and then, because it didn't seem like the people cared, I grabbed another. And I sank back in my chair and stared up at the blue sky and listened to the sound of the birds singing. They sang for five minutes straight, not missing a single note. I forgot about everything in those five minutes. Elder Pachis. The story. Mom. Being a soldier. Even Dad. Like this horrible fantasy took over. What if I could just never go back? Stay here on this island with the Flower Children. Eat fruit and flowers and drink ... well, whatever it was they drank. I'm sure it was delicious.

Would Mom eventually forget about me? Go on with her life? Maybe she could keep the farm. Maybe it would all work out if I just wasn't there.

I reached for another flower and listened to the birds for a few minutes. Their song echoed my thoughts.

"*Stay with us,*" they sang. "*Be free of your cares.*"

"I will," I said, living in the fantasy.

"*Never leave,*" they sang.

"I won't," I said.

And for a few more minutes our harmony went on.

"Another flower?" the girl said, handing one over to me.

I turned to look at her, even though that simple movement was a huge effort. All I wanted to do was keep looking up at the sky, listening to the birds, dreaming of a life with no cares at all.

"What?" I managed to say, because I was so far into the fantasy, that nothing else really made sense.

"A flower," she said, passing me another one.

I nodded slowly and held my hand out. And then I swiveled my head around since it was already moving and the momentum made it easier. Dory still sat next to me.

"I love this place," I said.

Dory didn't respond. He only stared ahead, not moving except for the slow movement of his mouth as he chewed yet another flower.

"Dory," I said. I angled forward so I could see his face.

"Eat your flower," the girl said.

It rested in my palm. I felt the small weight of it.

"Dory."

Still no response. And when I finally saw his face, I jumped back.

67

His eyes had turned from their normal dark green to the light, light blue of the Flower Children. And his face was the color of the ash from Mount Vesuvius.

I snapped my fingers in front of him. "Hey, Dory."

He acted like he didn't hear me or see me. All he did was chew.

"The flower," the girl said, closing my fingers over it.

My head snapped back to her. It was getting easier to move with every second that went by.

"I don't want the flower right now," I said, even though my tummy was still grumbling. I kinda did want the flower, except when I had the flower, all I wanted was the flower. It was a weird, endless loop.

"You need to eat the flower," she said, and her face shifted, just for a second. Her teeth looked rotten and had gaping holes where some of them were missing. And her hair, which I'd thought looked really pretty before, hung in limp strands around her face—her ashen face, the same color as Dory's. But the shift was so quick, that once she went back to normal, I figured I must've imagined it.

I leaned back in my chair. "I should probably write this all down."

She shook her head slowly. "You don't need to write it down."

The story. Elder Pachis. Mom. Our entire future was lost if I didn't come back with an epic tale. And then I thought about how much I missed Mom. How after Dad went away, before we found out he was missing, she'd tell me epic stories about him and all the heroic deeds he was off doing even though she had to be as worried about him as I was. I couldn't leave her alone. Not with him already gone.

"I do need to write it down," I said. "I really do. Everything depends on it."

"Nothing depends on it," she said. "Just let the future go. Relax. Have another flower."

Maybe she was right. Maybe I could let it go.

But Mom's face kept coming back to me. I could give up the future, maybe for myself, but not for Mom. Not when it mattered this much.

I stood, scooting my chair back. "I don't want another flower," I said, maybe too loud, because a bunch of the Flower Children swiveled their heads my way.

Okay, I didn't want to draw attention. This wasn't going well at all.

I sat back down. "I mean, I don't want it yet. I need to ... Do you guys have a bathroom?"

She nodded her head. "Of course. Follow me."

"No. No. No. Just point me in the right direction."

"You're sure?" she asked.

"Totally sure," I said.

So, she pointed back behind me, far into the city or village or whatever we were really in. All I'd seen were these outdoor tables and chairs.

"Come on, Dory," I said, grabbing his arm.

"He can stay," the girl said.

"He's coming," I said, and I yanked hard, pulling his skin.

It was the first time I noticed that Dory didn't have nearly as much hair on his arms as I did. It must be a puberty thing.

Dory didn't put up any kind of fight. He just let me pull him up and drag him through all the people. They were all acting weird, staring straight ahead, eyes crystal blue.

The bathrooms weren't hard to find. There were two of them, guys and girls, with signs marking which was which overhead. I started for the guys' bathroom, pulling Dory with me, but Dory pulled back.

"I have to go in this one," he said, pointing at the girls' room.

"That's for the girls," I said. "Come on."

"But I am a g …," he started, but then his words drifted off, like he suddenly remembered something.

"You are a what?" I said.

Dory's eyes were still unfocused, but it was like little thoughts were trying to go through his mind. They were just having a hard time.

"I'm a g … gorilla?" he said.

"You're a gorilla?"

He shook his head. "No. I mean I'm a gherkin."

"A gherkin? Dory, you aren't making any sense." What was in those flowers?

Wait. That was it. There was something in the flowers. Something affecting anyone and everyone who ate them.

"We need to get back to the ship," I said. "We need to warn Odysseus."

"Back to the ship?" Dory said. "Can't we stay here?"

"No. We can't stay here. We need to go." And I dragged him away from the bathrooms and back in the direction we'd come. Back to the beach. But before the boats or dock or anything came into view, there was Odysseus himself, on the path, talking to three ladies in togas.

They held a tray out in front of him, and he reached for one of the flowers on it.

I started running. "No! Don't eat it," I screamed, but I was still so far away.

He picked up the flower and seemed to consider it. And then he opened his mouth.

"Odysseus! Stop! You can't eat that!" I was closer now, and my voice must've carried across the wind to him because he hesitated and looked in my direction.

The three ladies turned my way, and as I got closer, their faces shifted. Ashen and dull with stringy hair and missing teeth and clothes that hung in rags. Their true appearance. Everything else was just an illusion.

"What do you say, Bard?" Odysseus called out to me.

"Don't eat the flowers," I said, and when I reached it, I smacked the tray to the ground.

"That was rude," Odysseus said.

"They're something in the flowers. Like poison. Or something. You can't eat it."

At my words, the three ladies took off, running back down the path. They didn't even cast Dory a second glance.

"Poison, you say?"

"Like a drug," I said. "It's making people not care about stuff."

"Is that why nobody has returned to the boat for nearly a week?" Odysseus said.

"Nearly a week! Are you kidding? It's been like a half hour." That was horrible news. The hourglass may be slowed down, but it was still ticking away the time I had left to get back to Ionia.

"A half hour," Dory said, finally coming up behind me. The focus was returning to his eyes, just like the color was returning to his face.

"No, young Bard. The entire lot of you has been gone for days."

This was not good.

"I've heard of this place," Odysseus said. "It is the Isle of the Lotus Eaters. People get trapped between the slices of time on this island. They never leave. It is a dangerous place."

That was a complete understatement.

"We need to get the guys and get out of here," I said. If we didn't do something, the guys were never going to want to leave.

"Exactly my thoughts," Odysseus said, and we set out back to the city of the Lotus Eaters.

"Don't eat any more flowers," I said to Dory once the people came into view. A bunch of them stood up and came our way with trays.

I ran straight for the table where we'd been sitting. But the girl was nowhere in sight. Instead there were a couple of kids that looked younger than me and Dory.

"Have you guys seen the girl that was here a few minutes

ago?" I said.

I wasn't sure if that was accurate. It could have been yesterday. If nearly a week had gone by, then my concept of time was way off.

They didn't respond. They only looked at me slowly with their blue eyes and went back to chewing the flowers. So I left them and dashed around the city, looking at every single person I could find. But the girl was nowhere. If I lost the scroll, I might as well jump off the nearest cliff. I had to have the scroll. There was no choice in the matter. And I was not going to give up looking for it.

"To the boats," Odysseus bellowed. I noticed he had Polites next to him, helping him gather up the guys. None of them seemed to want to go. But Odysseus was persuasive. I wasn't sure what he said to them, but slowly, one by one, they got up and started down the path. Maybe he promised them more flowers back on the boat.

I kept searching until I finally found her. She sat with Eurylochus, feeding him flowers. His normal dark polished skin was like ash. Maybe we could leave him here, leave him behind.

No, that was horrible. We couldn't leave anyone behind. Even if he was a moldy piece of bread.

"I need my scroll," I said to the girl.

"Why?" she said, like my statement confused her.

"Give it to me now." I didn't have time for games or questions.

"I don't have it." She pressed a flower to her cheek and let out a deep sigh.

I got right in her face. "You either find my scroll right this second, or I will find a way to destroy every single flower on this island. You will never have another one."

This was complete baloney. I had no clue how many flowers there were or how I'd destroy them. But the threat was enough. Her already wide eyes got wider, and she moved from table to table, searching for it.

I searched alongside her, and when she finally found it, under a beach umbrella, her face both relaxed and grew serious. She held it out to me and implored me with her eyes.

"Make us famous, Homer," she said. "Let the Flower Children be remembered. Let us be a warning to others."

The only person I planned to let read my story besides Dory was Elder Pachis, so I didn't think I'd be making anyone famous. But I nodded and took the scroll and ran.

Long story short. We all made it back to the boat. The men were seriously unhappy when they found out there weren't any flowers on board, and Odysseus had to tie them to the benches and make them not eat until they'd gotten all the flower out of their systems. They were furious until they weren't. And then they were just back to normal. I wrote it all down, as fast as I could, because I knew our journey would be ending soon. We were going to be to Ithaca in a matter of days.

A week later, we spotted a new island in the distance. I was sure it was Ithaca. Of course, once again, I was completely wrong.

INTO THE CAVE

I RAN TO THE GALLEY TO TELL DORY ABOUT THE island. Actually about the fact that the island wasn't Ithaca. Odysseus only had to glimpse the outline through the fog to make that assessment.

"We're not home, men," he'd said.

The guys let out a collective grunt of annoyance. And impatience. They'd been getting grouchier by the day. Four fights had broken out in the last two days alone. One nose had been broken.

"You promised us Ithaca," one of the stupider guys said. I think his name was Moronios or something like that. He never knew when to keep his mouth shut.

"And Ithaca I will give you," Odysseus said. "But not today."

"So where are we then, oh great king?" Eurylochus said,

sauntering over to stand next to Odysseus like they were equals. Odysseus didn't even look his way. "I've not seen this island before. We should investigate."

Here I'd hoped he'd say something along the lines of "we should proceed with caution and not attack the villagers" or "don't eat the flowers." But no, just a simple, "we should investigate."

"Should I go ahead and scout out the area?" Polites said.

Odysseus clasped him on the back. "No, my friend. We'll all go. This island looks fertile and green, and I feel good omens rippling off it."

The only thing I felt rippling off it was just one more delay before we got home. But fine, I totally understood that we needed more provisions. I just hated that every time we stopped for them, something went wrong.

"This time could be different," Dory said when I filled him in on what had happened above.

"You really think so?" I said.

"Yeah, sure," Dory said. "We've totally seen the worst of this trip."

So, I rolled up my scroll and refilled my pen with ink, and we set out, catching up to Polites once we got ashore. Rocks and shells littered the hillside, but we managed. He stopped every so often to pick up new shells for his braids since a bunch had come off in the last couple weeks.

Of course, some of the guys charged ahead, including Moronios. He kept saying, "First to the booty! First to the booty!" If anyone was listening, they'd know the Greeks had arrived.

"So this Ajax guy that Odysseus fought," I said. "Whatever happened to him?"

"He set out on his own ship," Polites said. "To return home to his father, King Telamon."

"King Telamon," I said. "No way! Our king is King Telamon, but he doesn't have any kids."

Polites shook his head. "Wrong you are, Homer. He has two sons, both heroes of the war with the Trojans."

That definitely wasn't right. It must be a different King Telamon we were talking about. Our king didn't have any living kids. Nobody to carry on the throne.

"How about others?" I said. "Were there any other Greek heroes?"

"Sure," Polites said. "There was Nestor and Peisistratus and Menelaus and Agamemnon. All great men. Oh, and Achilles. We can never forget Achilles."

"What about girls?" Dory said. "Were there any girls?"

Polites laughed. "Girls! War is no place for girls."

"But certainly there were some," Dory said. "Like maybe not in the actual fighting."

Polites cleaned some sand out of his eyepatch and readjusted it. "Well of course. There was Cassandra. And Clytemnestra. And Helen. Without Helen, the war never would have happened."

"She's the one who got kidnapped?" I remembered the guys

talking about her in the Horse.

"Yeah," Polites said, lowering his voice. "The guys aren't supposed to mention her. Makes Odysseus really upset."

"And why's that?" Dory said. "Is it just one more reason to not have girls in the story?"

I'd never quite realized what a feminist Dory was, but hey, I was cool with that. I was all about diversity in stories. I'd be happy to add some girls if they had a place in the story.

"It's because Odysseus didn't want to fight in the war in the first place," Polites said. "He wanted to be home, with his wife, Penelope, and his son, Telemachus. Newly born, just before the war started. He'd be over ten by now. But Agamemnon sailed up to the island one day and dragged Odysseus along."

"So why didn't Odysseus just say no?" I asked. It seemed simple enough to me. If you didn't want to fight, then why do it?

"Why are you here?" Polites said. "Did you choose this?"

I tossed a rock onto the beach far below as I thought about his answer. I wouldn't be here if Hermes hadn't sent me here. And Hermes wouldn't have sent me here if Elder Pachis hadn't told me I needed a story. And I wouldn't have needed a story if I'd done better in school. It was like a weird convoluted path arriving here, and in an equally convoluted way, I was completely responsible for it.

"I got in trouble," I said, which was as close to the truth as I could summarize. "This was my only choice."

"I figured," Polites said. "And for Odysseus it was much the same. This war was his only choice, no matter how much he may not have wanted it to be."

"So, what's up with his wife?" Dory said. "You think she's sitting home back in Ithaca waiting for him?"

"Doesn't matter what I think," Polites said. "Odysseus thinks she is, and he's going to return home to her no matter what."

"I think girls should be in stories more," Dory said. "They should be the main characters, not little supporting characters. It's like people think that if stories have girls in them, then guys won't read them, but that's totally not true. As long as the story is good, people will read it no matter what."

We crested the top of the hill we'd been climbing. We were super-far behind all the other guys who were running off toward the hills.

"Does Homer know?" Polites asked Dory.

Dory shot him a glance like he was about to skewer Polites with a spatula.

"Does Homer know what?" I asked. Seeing as how I was Homer, I figured if I knew what they were talking about, I'd be most suited to answer it.

"Nothing," Dory said.

"No, it's not," I said. "It's something. What is it?"

"It's nothing. I told you."

"Tell me now, or I stop teaching you to read and write," I said.

"You can't do that," Dory said. "You promised. And if you go back on a promise, you'll die a horrible torturous death."

"Whatever," I said. "Just tell me."

"There's no reason in keeping it a secret from Homer,"

Polites said. "He won't tell anyone."

"Right," I said. "I won't tell anyone." And then the weird little conversation we'd been having back on the Island of the Lotus Eaters came back to me. "Wait, does this have something to do with you being a grrrrr ..." What was it again? "A gorilla? A gherkin?"

Dory put his hands on his hips. "I'm not a gorilla, Homer. I'm a girl."

The trees. The birds. The air. Everything stopped moving.

"You're a what?" I said. Surely Dory had just told me he was a gorilla. Not what I thought I'd heard.

"A girl," Dory said. "You know, as in the opposite sex."

"Great Zeus!" I said. "That totally makes sense."

"What makes sense?" Dory said.

I motioned with my hand. "The way you stand. The way you roll your eyes. The way you stomp your foot when you're angry. You are a girl."

"Shhh ...," Dory said. "Don't say it so loud."

Polites was the only one around, so I wasn't worried about anyone hearing.

"And anyway, how do you know?" Dory asked Polites. "I've done a really good job keeping it a secret."

That was true. Well except for the little things I'd noticed. And the fact that Dory never went to the bathroom around any of the other guys. He—I mean she—always wanted privacy.

"Tessa told me," Polites said. "Back in Ismaros."

"Ugh, Tessa," Dory said. "She said she'd keep my secret."

"Well, why'd you tell her?" I asked.

"Girl stuff," Dory said.

I would have pried more, but that's when we heard laughter and shouts of joy coming from a cave in the hillside. It was only about fifty yards ahead, with a wide rounded opening about ten feet across.

The idea of going into a cave didn't seem like the smartest thing to me, and I guess it didn't to Odysseus either because he stood out front also, not entering.

"Don't tell anyone, Homer," Dory whispered as we hurried over.

Odysseus would have flipped if he'd found out. Girls on ships were bad luck. Everyone knew that. He'd blame everything that had happened so far on Dory.

"Is your name really Dory?" I whispered back. "That's a dude's name."

"It's short for Doryclus, and everyone thinks I'm a dude, so it's fine." Then she did that eye roll thing again.

"You need to keep it a secret," I said. "You can't let anyone find out."

"Duh, Homer," she said. "So just promise me you won't tell anyone."

"Duh," I said. "I'm not stupid."

"The men are inside?" Polites asked Odysseus as we hurried up to the cave. Odysseus wore his same yellow tunic, except it looked brand new, not torn in half like the last time I'd seen it.

I still couldn't believe Dory was a girl. Except I also could totally believe it. And now that I knew it, it was so obvious. But no one would find out because of me.

"Sounds like they found—" he started.

"We found booty!" Moronios said, running from the cave's mouth. In one hand he held a jug of what I guessed was wine since his mouth was stained bright red. In the other hand he held a huge hunk of bread with a few bites taken out. Around his neck were chains of gold.

"It looks like the mother lode," Odysseus said.

"We should take inventory," Dory said.

"A good plan," Odysseus said. "Cook, you lead the inventory."

"I don't think going in the cave is such a good idea," I said.

"Nonsense," Odysseus said. "There is no one about."

I had no plans to go into the cave. But then something let out a huge roar. I turned left, then right, but didn't see anything.

"Over there!" Dory said, pointing to the hillside in front of us.

Once I spotted it, I wanted to unsee it. Because coming up from the hill was a giant monster with a single eyeball in the center of his forehead sniffing the air and roaring. He took one look at us with that giant eye of his and started running directly toward us.

"Into the cave!" Odysseus shouted.

And since there was nowhere else to go, we ran into the cave.

The monster ran—

"Be specific, Homer," Dory said. "What kind of monster is

it? Details make every story better."

It wasn't really the time for details, but Dory was always right. I wonder if that had something to do with her being a girl.

"Fine," I said and scratched out the word "monster."

The hideous, half-dressed, hairy, slobbering cyclops ran directly toward the cave.

"Hide, men!" Odysseus cried.

The cave was huge and there were tons of rocks, so we all dashed behind them. The cyclops ran into the cave and looked around with that great big blue eye of his, and then it settled on one of the biggest rocks. He lifted it up—seriously, he lifted it with one hand; I don't think ten of Odysseus' men could have budged the thing—and then he placed it directly in front of the cave opening, blotting out all the sunlight.

We were trapped.

DINNER FOR THE CYCLOPS

TWO GUYS HAD BEEN HIDING BEHIND THE BIG ROCK. Moronios was one. Spitter was the other. Spitter wore the same red shirt every single second of every single day. When the cyclops picked up the big rock, they tried to dash around another one, but they weren't fast enough. The cyclops grabbed them with his huge hands. He raised Moronios to his mouth and bit him in half, squelching his screams before they even got started. I'd add more gory details, but it might not be appropriate.

As for Spitter, he started wiggling and squirming so violently, that the cyclops just squished him. Then he ate him.

(Insert more gory details here.)

(Redacted. Dory tells me that I shouldn't add any more, so we'll leave it at that.)

Odysseus was down two more men. Not that anyone was

going to much miss Moronios or Spitter, may they rest in peace in the cyclops's tummy.

The cave went silent. I don't think anyone even breathed. Nobody wanted to be noticed by the cyclops. And the cyclops … he seemed satisfied. He sat on a rock near the middle of the cave and slowly finished his dinner. The only sound echoing through the confined space, which felt smaller by the second, was the occasional belch and the crunching of bones.

"No gory details," Dory said.

I scratched out that part about the bones. The belching I left because burps are always funny.

"You're just grossed out because you're a girl," I said.

"Oh no, you don't," Dory said.

"Oh no I don't what?" I said.

"You don't make a single comment like that about me being a girl. That's exactly part of the reason why I've kept it a secret."

"Because people make girl comments?" I asked.

"All the time! About how girls aren't strong enough. Or how they aren't good at math, which, by the way, is the stupidest thing I've ever heard. I'm great at math. Stupid Demetrios can't add two numbers. And his dad wouldn't know how to balance his finances if he was down to four drachmas."

"I didn't say you weren't good at math," I said.

"You inferred that I was grossed out by things," Dory said.

"That's because it is gross," I said. "I'm grossed out. And seriously, how many bites does it take for him to finish his meal? He's been crunching for like ten minutes now."

"Maybe he got a bone stuck in his throat," Dory said.

"Possibly you two want to keep it down a bit?" Polites whispered from the next rock over.

But I guess it was too late, because that's when the cyclops picked me and Dory up and turned us upside down.

Which gets us back to the beginning of the story.

"Not the beginning of the story," Dory said. "We're well into the thick of things."

Yeah. True. So, we were upside down in the hands of the cyclops. My scroll and my pen fell to the ground. From behind the rocks, I could see all the guys looking up at us, but they kept their mouths shut. It was too late to point out that Dory and I should have done the same.

The cyclops lifted me close to his face. Way too close to his face. The stench rolled off his breath. If I didn't think of something quick, I was totally hosed.

"Wait a second," I said, hoping he understood Greek.

He cocked his head. "It speaks?"

"Yeah. Yeah. I speak," I said. Maybe that would be enough. He'd realize I was human and decide that it was completely inhumane to eat humans. Hence the word inhumane.

"Does it taste good?" he asked.

I shook my head, fiercely. "No. I taste horrible. Dreadful. I'm a total reject."

He narrowed that big eye at me. "How does it know?"

"Oh … well, you see … this other cyclops tried to eat me one time, and I tasted so awful that he spit me out whole. He brushed his teeth for five days straight after that. As he cursed the horrible taste in his mouth, he said the girl cyclopses would never like him if his breath smelled so bad. So, I highly recommend that you don't eat me."

"Hmmm …," he said. "Which cyclops tried to eat it?"

Oh, I hadn't thought of that. But it actually gave me a great idea. "He didn't tell me his name," I said. "Which was a huge mistake on his part. You see, I'm a storyteller. And the story I'm telling … well … It's going to be famous. Epic even. And I want you to be a huge part of that story."

"It wants me to be famous?" the cyclops said, and he batted his eyelid a few times as if this possibility had never occurred to him.

"Very famous," I said. "The most famous cyclops ever. What is your name?"

"Polyphemus," the cyclops said proudly, like it was the best cyclops name in the world.

"That's an amazing name," I said. "It will be perfect in my story."

"It will tell other cyclopses about me?" Polyphemus said. "Even girl cyclopses?"

I nodded, probably more enthusiastically than I needed to. But I was making progress. "Not just cyclopses. I'll tell the world. You, my friend, Polyphemus, will be remembered forever. But if you eat me, then I can't make you famous."

Polyphemus grinned. "I won't eat it. I'll eat the other one instead." And he raised Dory toward his mouth.

"No!" I said. "You can't eat her—I mean him either."

This genuinely seemed to confuse Polyphemus. "Why can't I eat it?"

The "tastes bad" excuse would only go so far, I knew.

"Because he's my editor," I said. "And if you eat my editor, then my stories will be awful. Sure, I can write them, but I completely need my editor to make them better. Editors are geniuses. They do magic with stories. Otherwise, stories die a long painful death, and no one ever reads them."

The cyclops thought hard, trying to find a hole in my logic. Or maybe trying to understand my logic at all. Dory kept shooting me dirty looks, like I should keep talking, but I figured I'd let Polyphemus puzzle this out.

"I won't eat it," Polyphemus said. "I want to be famous."

And he set us both on the ground.

"It will stay here," the cyclops said. "I will bring it some dinner. It will read me its story when I get back."

"Okay," I said, not sure what kind of dinner he had in mind.

He lifted the rock out from in front of the cave, and then left, resetting the rock from the outside. Which left me, Dory, Odysseus, and all the guys, except the two who'd been eaten, alive in the cave.

Odysseus slapped me on the back. "Good thinking, Bard. Make the cyclops famous. That's a quick mind you have."

Quick and desperate. It got my creative juices flowing. I grabbed my scroll and pen from behind a rock where they'd fallen and got to work on the story. Now it wasn't just the farm and my future on the line. It was my life. If the cyclops didn't like this story, I was going to be dead.

"That's his name, right?" Dory said, leaning over my shoulder. I'd just written Polyphemus.

"Yep," I said, scribbling frantically in the firelight. Polyphemus still wasn't back, and the guys had lit a fire and were roasting a sheep over it. Not the smartest of ideas. Odysseus, of course, had told them not to, but once the fire was lit and the sheep was dead, I guess he realized that he wouldn't really be able to hide all the evidence so he might as well enjoy some mutton, too. He sat off to the side of the group, whittling a long stick.

Dory sounded out words over my shoulder as I wrote. I was so into the words, that it didn't even bother me. It was like I'd entered some sort of magical writing zone. I only hoped it would be enough that Polyphemus would let me out so I'd have the chance to share it with the world. I tried to capture every detail. I also tried to embellish some of those details, describing what a great big strong, good-looking cyclops Polyphemus was. This was not true. Polyphemus smelled like he never showered. He looked like he never showered. I was pretty sure that he never had showered. But none of this needed to go into the story.

I was still scribbling when the scraping sound of the rock being moved echoed through the cave.

"Hide, men!" Odysseus shouted, but of course it was too late. The men sat around the fire with bellies full of roasted mutton.

"What is this?!" Polyphemus bellowed, and he grabbed one of the men—no clue what his name was; we'll just call him cyclops victim number three—and snapped his head off with his teeth.

We all shuddered from the noise.

"Don't you say a word," Dory said. "That wasn't the least bit gross."

But here's where things really got interesting. Polyphemus stepped closer to the fire, reaching for another of the guys. Odysseus—I guess he hadn't just been sitting there idle—grabbed the long stick he'd been whittling and raised it like a spear. The end was sharpened to a long spike.

He came from behind a rock and launched himself right at Polyphemus. The stick plunged forward. The spike went directly through the cyclops's giant eye.

"Ah!" Polyphemus cried, grabbing at the spear sticking out of his eye. "Where did the world go?"

The spear must've blinded him because once he yanked it out of his eye and threw it across the cave, he started flailing his arms around, knocking over rocks and stepping on sheep, and howling in pain. Two more guys got crunched in the madness. Cyclops victims four and five.

"What did it?" Polyphemus shouted. "What did this to me?"

"I did it," Odysseus yelled, stepping forward and sticking his hulking chest out like he'd solved all our problems.

"What is I?" Polyphemus cried.

"I am No One," Odysseus said.

"No One made the world go away," the cyclops cried. "Curse No One. I hate No One!"

"To the exit!" Odysseus yelled, and we all started running.

Minus points to Odysseus. The spear was smart. Not telling the cyclops his real name was smart. Announcing our exit strategy wasn't. Polyphemus floundered to the cave exit and positioned his giant body in front of it while he felt around for the rock. We were close to the exit now. Cupcake was nearly outside. We were all jealous until Polyphemus slammed the rock back into place, smooshing Cupcake and sealing us back into the cave. And then Polyphemus sank to the ground with his back against the rock and started crying, big slobbery tears that mixed with his blood and pooled down his face. I would've felt sorry for him except we were down six guys by now.

With him distracted and blind, we all ran back toward the rocks.

"Storyteller?" Polyphemus cried out, stopping me in my

tracks. He sniffed the air, almost like he could smell me.

I didn't say a word.

"Are you still there, storyteller?" he called, and then he sniffed loudly and cried anew. And I couldn't go any farther.

"I'm here," I said, stepping back toward him.

Dory grabbed my arm and tried to drag me to the back of the cave, but I shook her off.

"Tell me a story," Polyphemus said. "Please."

So, I sank to the ground in front of Polyphemus, and even though he couldn't see me, he could hear me. I told him about Ismaros. And about the island of the Lotus Eaters. And Tessa. And even of what I'd seen of the war, with the giant wooden horse. And Polyphemus listened until he stopped crying, and then he listened until he fell asleep.

CLOAKED IN MUTTON

"WE ATTACK AT DAWN," EURYLOCHUS SAID, TRYING
to sound like he was all in charge and stuff.

"We don't attack," Odysseus said.

"So you lead more men to their deaths?" Eurylochus said.

It got under my skin how he always challenged Odysseus.
Not that Odysseus was always right. But Eurylochus grated
on my nerves like two pieces of limestone rubbing against
each other.

"Why does Odysseus keep that guy around?" Dory asked
Polites. "He's so annoying."

Now that I knew Dory was a girl, she sounded more and
more like one. Like every phrase she said and the tones she
used in her voice. And I had to tell her about the hands on hips
thing. Guys just didn't do that.

"He's related to King Odysseus," Polites said. "A relative of the king's wife."

"Penelope," I said. "Right?" After Polyphemus had fallen asleep, I'd worked on filling in some of the details. Things like that. Turns out the guy in the red shirt who'd been eaten did have a name besides Spitter. It was Pyrrhus. Moronios was really Myronius. Cupcake was Stephanos. Odysseus promised we'd have a ceremony for the fallen once we were back on the ship.

"If we don't attack, then what do we do? Wait for it to eat all of us?" Eurylochus said.

"Of course not," Odysseus said, and that's when he told us the plan.

It was actually very clever. And took way more patience than I ever would have assumed Odysseus had. We waited until Polyphemus woke up, and then, like it was their morning ritual, the sheep all started making noise. They needed to go out to pasture. The first sheep wandered toward the front of the cave. Polyphemus pushed the giant stone out of the way, and then felt the top of the sheep, just to make sure it was a sheep and not one of us.

So, we all grabbed hold of a sheep, from underneath. Not a fun spot to be, but it fooled Polyphemus. He let every single sheep out, not realizing we all clung to their undersides. Once we were free of the cave, we ran, not looking back.

"To the boats!" Odysseus called.

What was it with this guy? Did he not learn the first time?

Of course, Polyphemus heard him. He erupted with terrible shouts and anger and started throwing rocks at us. We ran toward the ship, down the rocky hill. No one was worried about heading back to get any booty out of the cave. When we finally clambered aboard, the guys raised the anchors and we cast off, away from the rocky shore.

"Too bad, cyclops!" Odysseus shouted. "We've escaped your grasp. You'll have to find your dinner with no eye!"

It was completely unnecessary taunting.

"Tell me its true name," Polyphemus bellowed from the shore.

Odysseus laughed, bold and full of confidence. "I am Odysseus. King of Ithaca. Hero of the Trojan War. And you, blind cyclops, are no match for me."

Dory put her head in her hand. "Seriously? Maybe he should just draw the cyclops a map."

"I may be no match for it," Polyphemus shouted. "But Father is. Father will take care of it. Father will make it pay."

And the waves rose, making it abundantly clear who the cyclops's dad was: none other than Poseidon, god of the sea. Polyphemus threw rocks at our ships, and the waves tossed us around. I was sure we were dead at least five times. But the guys were determined. They rowed and rowed, and we finally got a safe distance from the island.

Odysseus strode up. Somewhere in the commotion, his yellow shirt had been torn once again, showing off his chest. "Well, that was close. But the worst is definitely behind us."

Good gods, this guy. I'd never seen someone so full of confidence, even in the eyes of a god's vengeance.

"Yep. The worst is definitely behind us." He flexed his muscles a few times for good measure.

I'd heard it before. I believed it less now than I had earlier. We were hosed. There was no getting around it. Making the gods mad was a really bad idea.

THE RAINBOW
SPARKLE CLUB

THE GOOD NEWS WAS THAT I HADN'T EVEN HAD TO
flip the hourglass once yet. It was still draining, but I had more
than enough time. Time was flowing differently somehow.
Like the guys were all getting shaggy, but my hair and fingernails hadn't grown even a speck. Neither had Dory's. Whatever
Hermes had done to the hourglass, time was in our favor. So,
I didn't mind the fact that we drifted on the ships for a while.

Dory got super creative for mealtime and taught a bunch
of the guys to fish. I continued teaching her to read and write,
all the while going back through the story, adding little details here and there. The colors of the lotus flowers (aubergine
and emerald, which are really just fancy names for purple and
green). The weather on Ismaros (dreary and dismal). The infernal sea that stretched in front of us.

"Infernal is a good word," Dory said. She used the golden paint to draw on the walls of the storage room, writing out each letter.

"You think so?" I'd been about to scratch it out since it kind of conjured up a fiery image in my mind.

"Sure," Dory said. "It's like irritating, tiresome, hellish."

That did fit the sea pretty well. We'd been rowing in circles for days. The bright blue sails, not quite as bright as they'd been before, hung limp in the air.

"We need wind," Odysseus said, stomping across the deck. He'd been doing that more and more as the days went by. The men kept their distance.

"There is no wind," Eurylochus said in his whiny weasel voice. The more I hung around him, the more he reminded me of Demetrios from back at school, like they both thought they were better than everyone else. It was almost like there was a special training class snobby people went to in order to get better at being snobs.

"That is apparent and thus unnecessary for you to point out," Odysseus said. "Which is why I stated that we need wind. A simple fact. And unless you have a solution to the simple fact that we need wind, then I suggest you keep your mouth shut."

Odysseus was not a hothead. This was about the closest he came to actually fighting with anyone on board.

Eurylochus stepped back. He wasn't a complete idiot. At least not all the time. "Of course, great King Odysseus. But we should have wind. It's not right. Something is giving us bad luck."

I forced myself not to look at Dory. If anyone found out she was a girl, they'd blame her for our lack of wind for sure. Girls on ships definitely equaled bad luck.

"Bard, where do I get wind?" Odysseus said.

There was plenty of wind onboard since we'd been eating a ton of stored beans, but I kept my sarcastic thoughts to myself.

"I'm not sure." I almost answered him in Dactylic Hexameter out of habit except then I remembered at the last minute that it kind of annoyed Odysseus.

"Not sure?" Odysseus said. "Have you told no great stories of men and wind before?"

The only stories I'd told of men and wind were stupid jokes that I knew Odysseus would not find humorous right now. I sifted through my memories from back in school, wishing I'd stayed awake for more of the boring lectures Elder Pachis insisted were important. There'd been lectures on math and science of course, but also other lectures, like about all the different gods and what they protected.

I put my hand up because something tickled the back of my brain. "There's a god of wind," I said. "No, that's not quite right. There is a Keeper of Wind. Yes, the Keeper of the Winds. What's his name? It has like a million vowels in it."

"Aeolus," Polites said, limping over to join us. "But I've heard he's pretty stingy when it comes to protecting the wind. Doesn't like to part with it."

Odysseus waved his hand as if this last part was of little

consequence. "We'll deal with that when the time comes."

What this meant was that Odysseus would try to steal the wind from Aeolus if he didn't give us any. Just like back on Ismaros.

"How do we find this Keeper of the Wind?" Odysseus said.

Little bits and pieces of the lore started coming back to me, almost like Elder Pachis was next to me, whispering in my ear.

"Oh, I know," I said. "We look for the floating island of Aeolia."

"Floating island." Odysseus narrowed his eyes. "There is a lot of sky. How would we find a floating island?"

Polites pointed to his good eye. "I can spot it. I can spot anything."

"But how will you know where to look, man?" Odysseus said. I could tell from the edge of hope that crept into his voice that he wanted to believe Polites and he wanted to believe me.

"Gods love when you pray to them," Dory said. "Also offerings. Gods love offerings. So, we make a couple offerings—oh, but not food; we're short on food."

Odysseus looked closer at Dory. I held my breath, sure at any second every single person on board would realize Dory was a girl.

If Odysseus had any clue, he didn't let on.

"Prayers and offerings," Odysseus said. "We can do that. Men, we pray!"

So, the guys all prayed, and we cut open a bunch of pillows and threw the feathers into the sky. And on the second day,

Polites spotted the floating island.

It hung in the clouds above us, like a cloud itself, with golden ladders made of silk rope hanging down. Odysseus took these ladders to be a good sign. An invitation. He ordered the anchoring of all twelve ships, and then we climbed up the long ladders to the floating island. It took a little convincing for me to get Dory to climb, especially once we were halfway up, since she didn't seem to do so well with heights, but then the wind started blowing and swinging the ladders back and forth which helped convince her to keep moving.

Steep cliffs made completely of bronze surrounded the island, but even these had ladders, as if whoever lived up above—I was really hoping it was Aeolus at this point—was happy to have guests come visit.

So, we climbed some more ladders until we got to the top of the bronze cliffs. And there, like something out of a fairy tale, sat an enormous palace made of the same bronze.

"Men, we're in the right place," Odysseus said, and then he strode forward, making it abundantly clear that he, of all the guys, was in charge. Dory and I hurried up next to him. I got these kinds of special privileges since I'd promised to make him famous. Not that I got this fame thing. Why did everyone want to be famous? I found pleasure in knowing that after I died, no one would remember my name.

As we got closer to the palace, the drawbridge lowered, and the gate opened. A huge bunch of kids came running out. They all looked like they were about the same age as Dory and me, half were guys, half were girls, they sported every skin color from pitch black to albino, and they were dressed in togas the colors of the rainbow. That actually made it pretty easy. There was a guy and a girl in red, a guy and a girl in orange, and so on all the way through purple.

"Visitors!" the girl in the yellow toga squealed, and she clapped her hands together like we were the most exciting thing to happen around here in years.

"Visitors!" the others all echoed.

"My name is King Odysseus," Odysseus said. "I've come to speak with Aeolus, Keeper of the Winds."

On cue, one of our guys let out a huge fart that ripped through the air.

All twelve kids started giggling. Fourteen if you counted me and Dory.

"Dory and me," Dory said. "When are you going to get that right?"

"It's tricky," I said.

"You're not trying, Homer," Dory said, but I waved away her comment.

"Dad! Some king is here to see you!" the girl in blue hollered in a voice so loud, I wanted to cover my ears. It floated through the air, almost like the sound itself was alive.

Odysseus raised an eyebrow, just barely. *Some king.* He probably didn't like that very much. But Aeolus was a god, and thankfully Odysseus kept his mouth shut.

Their dad must've heard, because he came striding out the

main gate with a huge grin on his face. He looked older than Elder Pachis which, until this very moment, I'd thought was impossible.

"Odysseus. King of Ithaca! How wonderful of you to visit my humble island," the guy said. It didn't take a genius to put one and one together. This old geezer was Aeolus, Keeper of the Winds.

"We prayed to find your island," Odysseus said. "We—"

But Aeolus cut him off. "Not yet. Not yet. We must save the story."

"But we need—" Odysseus started again.

"Food," Aeolus said. "You need food. And I have food."

At that, all the guys let out an uproarious cheer since we'd been eating nothing but eel for the last five days. Aeolus stepped aside and let them file into the palace. Me, Dory, and Polites stood aside.

"Dory, Polites, and I," Dory said.

I put up my hand. "No more. I'll fix it later." I wanted to get the story out. There would be plenty of time to revise it once it was done.

"You think it's safe in there?" I asked Polites. I didn't want to risk losing my scroll yet again. I'd already had two close calls.

Polites narrowed his good eye. "How about I go in and check it out? You stay here, and I'll come get you."

"No way, dude," the boy in green said, stepping forward. "They can hang with us while you old people talk."

That actually sounded way better than listening to a bunch

of boring grown-up talk.

Polites looked them once over and then must've decided that the twelve kids looked harmless enough. "Holler if you need me. I'll find you." And then he followed behind the guys who'd just about all made it through into the palace.

"I'm Homer," I said, giving him a small little bow. Is that what you did for gods? Bow to them? Were these kids gods? They looked like some kind of rainbow sparkle club.

"I'm Dory," Dory said. "Short for Doryclus."

The blue boy frowned. "That's a boy's name."

"So what?" Dory said and put her hands on her hips like she was daring him to say anything else about it.

"No worries, little dudette," the blue boy said. "We're casual here on Aeolia. I'm Alpha, and these are my brothers and sisters. Beta. Gamma. Delta. Epsilon." He continued through the alphabet all the way to Lambda, pointing at each brother and sister in turn. I wasn't sure I'd remember who was who, but at least I'd remember the names.

"You guys hungry?" Beta said, stepping forward. She was the girl in red, and, okay, I know I shouldn't be thinking about stuff like this, but she was super cute. She had really dark skin and dark brown eyes and curly hair with light ends that seemed to catch the sunlight, and she had a smile that made my insides melt.

"We're really hungry," I managed to say.

Dory elbowed me.

"Come on, then," Gamma, the guy in orange, said.

"Follow us."

So, we followed them into the palace. I checked around but didn't see Odysseus and his men anywhere. The kids led us to a great big atrium with a ton of chairs and big fire pits and plants and some contraption that a few of them kicked their sandals off and started bouncing on.

"Cool place," I said. The farm where Mom and I lived was nothing like this. Sure, I goofed around plenty at home, but it was mostly climbing olive trees and hiding out in the barn when it was time for cleaning up after the chickens.

We sat around and told stories and joked about breaking wind. And we grilled fluffy sugary lumps that melted in my mouth when I ate them. And even when night came, we stayed up late because I hadn't had such a good time since this whole adventure began. Beta sat super close to me and laughed at all my jokes. Which was totally cool. What wasn't so cool was that Alpha sat equally close to Dory. So, I scooted away from Beta and closer to Dory.

I asked about Odysseus the next morning.

Epsilon shook his head. "Our dad is the slowest man in the universe. They'll be negotiating for weeks."

"Weeks!" I said. "Are you kidding? I have to get this story back to Elder Pachis like yesterday." I held up the hourglass, showing how little sand was left in it. I'd probably have to flip it in the next day or two, but they didn't know that I still had nine more rotations before it was due.

Beta placed her hand on my arm, and it kind of made me

feel all goofy inside. "But your story's not done."

I unrolled the scroll, showing off all the words that I'd written. "What are you talking about? My story's way done. Everything I'm adding now is just a bonus."

She leaned over and looked at the words, reading them slowly. After a few minutes, she looked up. "Where's the climax? How does the story end?"

"Well, the Greeks won the war. With the horse. See, right here." I pointed to the tiny picture I'd drawn to go along with the words.

"That's not the end," she said. "Odysseus isn't home yet."

"That's not my problem," I said. "I didn't sign on to write some bibliography about his royal highness."

"Biography," Dory said.

"Whatever," I said. "That's not my job."

"You're wrong, Homer," Beta said.

I wanted to disagree, except she was really cute and I kind of liked her, so I just shrugged and said, "Maybe."

"But anyway, what you have so far is really good," she said. "You're a great writer."

I laughed aloud even though her words made me all warm inside. "Yeah, whatever."

"No, I'm serious," Beta said. "In fact, we should go show this to my dad."

Of course, her eleven brothers and sisters all agreed with her, so they dragged me and Dory back into the palace, down about fifty corridors painted in rainbow colors, until we came to a room where Odysseus sat with Aeolus.

Things were not going well. Odysseus had his head in his hands as if he were trying to hold all his frustrations inside.

"Dad," Beta said. "Homer is a storyteller."

Aeolus' eyes immediately perked up. "A storyteller?"

She nodded, her eyes wide. "I read his story. It's really great. You should hear it."

Which is how I got roped in to telling him story after story after story. I read from the scroll first—making sure to edit out the parts about Dory being a girl. And when I finished reading and our stories had come to an end, he asked for more. So, I started telling stories of the gods. And when those ran out, I started making stuff up. Stories about cyclops romances. Lotus Eater fight clubs. I spun the stories out of control, sure he'd call me out on them and demand to have my head cut off or something like that. But Aeolus and all twelve kids hung on my every word. They laughed until they cried, and they cried until I made them laugh again. I wanted to do this forever.

"Yes! Wonderful!" Aeolus cried. "You have given me stories like none I have ever heard before. And for this I am eternally in your debt."

Now that made Odysseus smile. And the negotiations went great from there. Sure, an entire month went by, but at the end of the month, we had provisions for the boat and a bag holding back all the winds that we didn't want.

"Take this bag, King Odysseus," Aeolus said. "And keep it tightly closed. Only the westward wind is not trapped inside.

So long as you keep the bag closed, that westward wind will bring you home."

Home would be good. I was definitely ready to get to Ithaca then back to Ionia and be done with this entire journey.

"I'll miss you," Beta said, and she leaned forward and gave me a kiss on the cheek.

I must've turned the color of a poppy. But it left me smiling the entire trek back down the ladders and to the ships.

"Nobody opens this bag," Odysseus said, holding it high for all the guys to see.

"Does it have mead in it?" the guy we called Rum said.

"No mead," Odysseus said.

"Then don't worry," Rum said. "We won't touch it."

Then the westward wind started blowing. The ships began to rock on the sea. We raised our anchors, dropped our sails, and set our course for Ithaca.

SKELETONS IN THE CLOSET

EURYLOCHUS WAS BEHIND IT. I KNOW HE WAS. IT was just one more way for him to cause dissent among the guys in the hope that they'd revolt against Odysseus and maybe put him in charge. He started telling the guys that there was gold inside the bag. Which was not true. There was a bunch of wind. A worthless bag full of wind. And even if there was gold, it's not like the bag was all that big. I guess that's what made it easy to steal.

Whoever it was waited until we'd sailed for nearly a week. And then, while everyone slept, somebody stole the bag from Odysseus. I wasn't awake, of course. I was peacefully sleeping in the storage room with my head on a bag of grain, listening to the wind in the sails and the water lapping up against the side of the ship, but I could almost imagine that person grinning with glee once they got the bag. Then they took it to a far corner of the deck and opened it.

The sun was just coming up in the east, and Odysseus shouted, "There she is! The beautiful shining star of Ithaca! Men, we are home!"

I barely got a glimpse of Ithaca as I ran to the deck. Dory was already awake, up there watching. On the horizon sat a green, lush island, sparkling in the morning light. Ithaca! After so long. And from here, I'd be able to take my story and go home.

The men erupted with cheers, but their cheers were drowned out as the wind started to howl. And the sky darkened and the clouds swirled. And the wind that had been pushing us toward Ithaca turned. The men ran to the oars and pulled against the water, but it was no use. The eastward and southward and northward winds blew, and nothing, not even the strength of fifty men rowing, was enough.

Ithaca slowly drifted out of sight, and the ships rocked on the waves. The guys rolled up the sails to keep them from tearing in the torrential wind, and then we tied down everything and hid below deck.

I don't know. I lost count. But it felt like the wind blew us for years. I know it wasn't that long. It was maybe only a few days. A week. But at the end of the week, when the winds finally settled down after their escape from the bag, Ithaca was gone. So were my dreams of getting home to Mom anytime soon.

Of course, nobody 'fessed up to opening the bag. We found it discarded in a heap on the deck. We also found holes in the sails, torn by the fierce wind. Odysseus prayed to Aeolus again, begging the Keeper of the Winds to gift us again. We threw offerings over the side, but the floating island never appeared. We were on our own.

Ψ

A MONTH WENT BY WITH NO LAND. NONE. LIKE NOT even a rocky little hill in the middle of nowhere. And yes, our food ran short. Dory had the men fishing every other day. And on the days they weren't fishing, she had them cutting and drying the fish so it would stay edible. She was also onto this whole seaweed kick. The stuff tasted like mud flavored taffy, but she insisted that it had lots of nutrients since it lived in the sea.

After the month, we finally spotted land. Polites yelled from up in the crow's nest, but then he hurried down as much as his leg would let him.

"It's very rocky," he told Odysseus. "I've never seen such terrain."

"Bard," Odysseus said.

I hurried over to him with my scroll and pen.

"What do you know of a rocky island to the west?" he asked.

Had he not figured out yet that I knew a whole bunch of nothing? It was like Odysseus thought this storyteller thing gave me some sort of eternal knowledge. This was the first story I'd ever written.

"Not much." I didn't want to muster up the effort to make him think I knew what I was talking about.

"No stories of a rocky island?" he asked.

I shook my head. "Not yet. But I'll be sure to record every detail."

"Good," Dory said. "I love how you're taking initiative like that."

I didn't bother responding, but it was funny how the more details I added, the better the story got.

"I've heard rumors of a rocky island," this guy everyone called Fish said, wandering over with another guy. We called the second guy The Guy Who Hangs out with Fish since they were always together. Fish had a giant piece of—you guessed it—fish wrapped in seaweed on a stick, and grease dripped down his beard. It was like hygiene was the last concern of anyone onboard.

Odysseus turned to the guy. "What rumors, Fish?"

Fish stood up a little straighter and wiped his chin with his sleeve. "It is an island protected by sharks. Inhabited by flesh eaters. They drink the blood of their victims and build houses from their bones."

The Guy Who Hangs out with Fish said, "Do they have anything to eat besides fish and seaweed on the island?"

Seriously? What was wrong with this guy? He'd just heard about blood sucking cannibals, and he wanted to hang out and have afternoon tea with them?

"We should be cautious," Odysseus said.

"We should check it out," The Guy Who Hangs out with Fish said.

"Do you think they've spotted us yet?" Fish asked.

Polites shook his head. "We're still pretty far out. If we wait until it gets dark, we can slip up to the shore and hide in the coves."

So that's what we did. All twelve boats anchored until the sun went down. Then, under the cover of darkness, we rowed until we neared the rocky shore. Of course, the cove that we found was only big enough for one ship. Our boat moved into the cove, and the others anchored as near to the rocks as possible without actually smashing into them. The guys were most excellent sailors, as much as I like to point out their less redeeming qualities.

Odysseus picked three guys to go check out the alleged vampire flesh eaters. Since Fish seemed to be the local expert on this place, he went along with Eurylochus and Polites.

I grabbed my scroll and filled my pen with fresh ink.

"What do you think you're doing?" Dory asked.

"Going with them," I said.

"No, you're not," Dory said. "Did you not hear the part about the cannibals?"

I laughed. "Like that's true. That completely has to be an urban legend. Cannibals? And blood drinkers? Who does that? That's crazy talk. I'm going to get the real story. And I certainly can't trust these guys to get it for me."

"What if it's not an urban legend and they eat you for breakfast?"

"People don't eat people," I said. "That's just weird."

113

"Then why is there even a word like *cannibal?*" Dory said.

It was a good point. I hated to admit that.

"That's the kind of word parents make up to scare their kids at night. Like boogeyman. Or Chupacabra. They aren't real."

"Whatever, Homer," she said and grabbed an empty sack from the storeroom.

"What are you doing?" I asked.

"Coming with you," Dory said.

"No, you're not."

Dory crossed her arms. "If you go, I'm going."

"It's not safe," I said.

"You just said it was," Dory said.

"I meant that it was safe for me, not for a gi—"

"You better be saying gorilla," Dory said. "Now let's go."

There was no arguing with Dory. But I also wasn't willing to stay here and miss out on the story.

We trailed after the three guys, staying far enough away that we could hide if we needed to. Fish led the way, like some kind of brave explorer. He took a path up the rocky hillside until he came to a well. And at the well, was a super cute girl with short blond hair and a bright red dress and gold necklaces and bracelets covering her.

She saw all of us approaching, even me and Dory, since it was too late to hide by the time we saw her. A giant smile beamed on her face, and she waved.

"Hi!" she said, hurrying over toward us. "It's so nice to see you!" Her words were so bubbly, they almost popped out of

114

her mouth.

"We come in peace," Fish said.

It was such a dorky thing to say. I wanted to crawl under a rock.

The girl giggled. "Of course you do. Lamos is a peaceful island. The city of Telepylus where I live has remained at peace for centuries. Centuries. That's a really long time."

Eurylochus elbowed Fish. "See, I told you there were no cannibals here."

Confusion clouded the girl's face. "Cannibals?"

Polites shook his head. "It's nothing. So, this is Lamos?"

"Sure," the bubbly girl said. "You'll love it here. Come on. I'll take you to meet my dad. He's the king. That means he's important. Really important."

"Maybe we should get King Odysseus," Fish said. "You know, because kings like to meet other kings. They can do kingly things."

"You're not alone?" the girl said.

"Oh, no," Fish said. "There are a whole bunch of us. Twelve whole ships of fifty men each."

"That is so many people," the girl said. "Like a whole lot. Now come on."

She led us down through a valley and up to the top of another hill. I kept waiting to see some magnificent palace like Aeolus had, so when we came to this hovel that looked like it had been carved out of the hillside, I was a little surprised.

"Where's the palace?" Fish said.

She grabbed his arm and squeezed it, like she was feeling how strong he was. "This is the palace. My family loves the earth. Really loves it. We're all about recycling and stuff like that. But I'm sure my parents, you know, the king and queen, can tell you way more about that. They know everything. Everything."

If that was true, if they really knew everything, maybe they could also tell us the fastest way to Ithaca.

We went inside the rock palace. There was a bench not far from the door, so I sank down and started writing. I didn't want to forget all this stuff. Dory plunked down next to me.

"I love how concerned they are about recycling," she said. "We should do more of that on the ships." She hated how the guys just tossed the bones and skin and everything overboard when they were done. According to Dory, there were a million uses for things like that.

The three guys went ahead with the girl to meet the king and queen. I wrote down all the noteworthy things about the island, like the recycling thing and the cave palace. At least we'd debunked the urban legend. Once I was done, I sat my pen down on the bench beside me. Except it left a huge dark smear, and I tried to wipe it up. But the more I tried, the deeper into the bench it went. And the bench was bright white. Gods above, I hoped no one would notice.

But then I looked a little closer at the bench. At the edges.

"Dory," I said.

"Yeah?"

"What does this bench look like it's made of?"

Dory skinned fish every day. She knew in a second. "Bones," she whispered, and that's when we heard the scream.

We bolted up from the bench and ran down the hall, looking for a place to hide. There was a doorframe made from more bones, but I wasn't going to let that stop me. We dashed inside, narrowly avoiding footsteps from out in the hall. They pounded on the floor, like elephants. I dared to peek, then I wished I hadn't.

Twenty giants marched past. Like real giants. Sure, they looked kind of like me and Dory in that they had two arms and two legs and a head. That sort of thing. But they were twice as tall as us and had teeth that had been sharpened into spikes.

"They must be around here somewhere," one of the giants said, a lady giant, I think. "She said she left them in the entryway."

Fires of Hades, they were looking for us. We ducked back into the room where we hid. My heart pounded so hard, I was sure it would give our hiding place away. But then everything got really quiet all of a sudden. We dashed out.

"We need to find the guys," Dory said.

No sooner were we out in the hallway, the scream came again, but was quickly squelched, like someone had … Well, I didn't want to hypothesize. Turns out the truth was worse than anything I could have imagined.

"Run, young friends!" Polites yelled, coming around the corner, his long braids flying behind him. "Run as fast as you can!"

From the way he ran, no one would have ever guessed that he had a bum leg. Eurylochus wasn't far behind him.

We dashed from the palace, but the giants were right on our heels.

"They ate Fish! The Laestrygonians. They ate Fish!" Eurylochus screamed, shoving his way past us all. "The queen. She drank his blood!"

That explained why Fish wasn't with them. I felt kind of sad for Fish but also really happy for myself that I was still alive. I didn't want to be eaten by cannibals.

"Make for the ships!" Polites said, and we bounded down the rocky shore.

The giants didn't follow us. Instead, they picked up humongous rocks and threw them. The rocks smashed down the hillside, barely missing us. They bounced and flew through the air and smashed into the boats below. We ran so fast, I was sure that I'd lose my balance and tumble to my death if a rock didn't hit me first, but we made it to the bottom and ran for the cove.

"Cast off!" Polites cried, and Odysseus commanded his men into action.

But then I tripped on a rock, and my scroll slipped from my hand, falling down a crevasse. I hurried to my feet and leaned over, reaching my hand as far into the hole in the ground as I could. I almost had it. Just a little bit more.

"Come on, Homer!" Dory called. She and Polites and Eurylochus were already on board, and the ship was pulling away from the cove quickly. But I was not leaving without this scroll. I might as well be eaten by these Laestrygonians. I stretched the tiniest bit more. My fingers brushed against the edge of the scroll and then curled around it. Success!

I tucked it under my arm and ran. Already the ship was ten feet away. They were leaving without me. I was not going to make it. And to make matters worse, sharks surfaced in the water. I couldn't wade through it or swim. One shark spotted me. It opened its mouth and waited.

I backed up, and with a running start, I ran for the water, and I jumped.

An eternity passed as I flew through the air. I was sure I wasn't going to make it. The scroll started to slip from under my arm, but I clenched it down, holding it in place. If I survived, I was taking this scroll with me.

My feet landed hard … on solid deck. I fell to the wood and kissed it, not caring that it looked completely stupid. I was alive. But that wasn't true for so many others. No other ships pulled out of the harbor. Ours was the only one left.

CHEESEBURGER
IN PARADISE

IN THE DAYS THAT PASSED, I TRIED NOT TO THINK OF the guys on the other eleven ships. It wasn't easy, losing that many people. I didn't know most of their names. That didn't matter. They were still friends. Companions on our journey. But when I did think of them—when I thought of the ships— here's what I imagined.

Their sleek black ships sailed through the water, bright blue sails billowing in the wind. The breeze carried them down the River Styx and across to the Elysian Fields. And when they disembarked, all their loved ones stood there waiting for them. Their children ran to them. Their wives embraced them. The sun shone in the sky overhead. Ladies walked around with trays of food, huge hunks of meat dripping with melted cheese piled high on bread, deep fried potato slices, and gelato. And the guys were content. Truly at peace.

But I tried not to think about it very often.

GOING PORCINE

I LOST TRACK OF TIME. SAND SLIPPED THROUGH THE hourglass, still on its second rotation. But since the hourglass was Ionia time, not the time we were really in, I made marks on the scroll, counting days, then weeks. Then the weeks turned into months. We sailed across the sea, never spotting land. Never spotting anything. Until one day, Polites shouted from the crow's nest. Finally. Something.

No, it wasn't Ithaca. Even I knew that. I'd seen a glimpse of Ithaca before the winds blew us away. But on this shore, the beach was white sand, and the sun was shining, and best of all, even from out on the water, the guys spotted the herds of animals roaming around. Gazelles and deer and antelope.

"We're eating venison tonight!" this guy we called Ear shouted. Ear lost his—you guessed it—left ear back in Troy, hence the nickname. Supposedly he'd lost it not while fighting against the enemy but in a bet against friends. Or I guess they weren't really friends since they made good on the bet.

My stomach growled in reply. The thought of something— anything—besides fish and seaweed was enough to make me want to jump overboard and swim for shore immediately. Except then I remembered the sharks. I planned to never jump a shark again in my life.

Everywhere we'd been, something had gone wrong. Well, except for the floating island. I'd go back there any day.

"You're just saying that because Beta kissed you," Dory said.

"Not true," I said, though I was pretty sure I turned bright red. The same color as Beta's dress. I shook my head to clear the image.

"She kissed you on the cheek," Dory said. "I saw it."

"That doesn't count," I said. "A tiny peck on the cheek is not a real kiss."

This was a complete lie. It felt like a real kiss. Not that I'd had a lot of real kisses to compare it to. Okay, none. But I didn't write that down because when Elder Pachis read this story, he had no reason to know anything about the lack of my love life.

Eurylochus and Odysseus noodled over who should go ashore. They both wanted to lead the expedition, and since they were both more stubborn than minotaurs, neither would give in. So finally, they drew straws to decide. Eurylochus won.

"I'll take twenty men and Polites," Eurylochus said. "We'll search the island. Decide if it's safe."

"Bring the bard," Odysseus said. "And the cook."

After the cannibals thing, a big part of me never wanted to leave the ship again. But if I stayed here instead of going along, I'd have to depend on Eurylochus for secondhand information. I didn't want to depend on him for anything.

I gave a half-hearted attempt to convince Dory to stay on board, but she completely ignored me. So the twenty guys, Dory, Eurylochus, Polites, and I set out on a small boat and landed on the beach.

Immediately the animals started for us. That's when we discovered our mistake. The animals weren't all a bunch of veggie eaters like we'd thought. Lions and wolves joined the herd.

Eurylochus pulled out his sword. "Behind me, Bard."

I was glad he valued my life. Or maybe he just wanted to be made famous also.

But the lions and wolves didn't attack. Instead they walked forward and started rubbing up against the guys like they wanted their heads scratched. The guys looked from one to another, and then a couple of them did start scratching the animals between the ears.

"Are you getting all this, Homer?" Dory asked.

I scribbled on the scroll, making notes that I'd fill in later.

"Do we bag some venison?" one guy we called Pork asked. In all fairness, he'd lost a ton of weight since we started the journey. Next to him, Ear nodded enthusiastically in agreement.

Eurylochus put up a hand. "Not yet. Let's use caution and see what we find on this island. I feel strange magic in the air."

It was maybe the most sensible thing I'd ever heard Eurylochus say. I guess without Odysseus right here next to him, he didn't have to worry about trying to outdo the king. But I was glad he wanted caution. Something floated through the air that made me feel like I'd fallen into a world crafted of fantasy. Something that made my skin tingle.

We pushed forward from the beach and into the trees. The animals loped all around us, some following behind, some nearly leading us. All the while Dory made her own notes on a scrap of smooth wood she'd turned into an erasable board.

"There's fruit. And honey. And vegetables," she said, writing it all down. "And these animals. Which ones do you think would taste the best?"

I swear half the animals looked her way, almost like they understood her words. Except that was completely ridiculous. Animals might be smart, but they didn't know Greek from Pig Latin.

"Antelope?" I said. I didn't really know. I'd grown up with farm animals like chickens and cows which made up the bulk of my meat.

Dory wrote *antelope* down on her list and underlined it.

"Your handwriting is really getting good," I said.

"My handwriting is better than yours now," she said.

I didn't argue because in the last months, I'd learned that arguing with Dory never resulted in victory.

"You see that through the trees," Pork said to Eurylochus, pointing.

Eurylochus stopped walking. "I see it. A building."

"A palace. They're gonna have some good grub," Pork said, and he ran forward before anyone could stop him.

"Pork, come back," Eurylochus hissed, but it was no use. Pork had disappeared through the trees.

We waited, held our breath, inched forward, until finally his voice drifted back through the trees.

"You guys have to see this," Pork called.

"Caution," Eurylochus said, and the guys moved forward.

We came out of the trees into a garden with flowers and bees and animals and grass so green it looked like sparkling jewels. Across the green grass was the palace, crafted entirely of crystal, like something out of a fairy tale. In front of the palace stood Pork next to a woman with pale skin who didn't have nearly enough clothes on, and what she did have on were kind of a little see-through. A lot see-through. Her long blond hair hung over her shoulder, covering some of her up, but not enough to keep me from blushing furiously. Her pale hand rested on Pork's head, and he stared at her like she was some sort of angel sent to rescue him.

"What brings ya here?" the woman said, drawling the words while at the same time running them all together.

Eurylochus took charge, stepping forward. A giant wolf flanked him, but he ignored it.

"We've come for food and rest," he said. "Stopping by on our way home to Ithaca."

"Pretty far from Ithaca, aren't ya?" the woman said.

I cringed. I was glad Odysseus wasn't here to hear that.

"We got a little lost," Eurylochus said. "Our king doesn't know what he's doing."

I cringed more at this. Odysseus would cut out Eurylochus' tongue for that kind of insult.

"Is that so? Well maybe I can help ya find the way," the woman said. "And if ya know the way, then maybe ya don't need this king of yours after all."

Caution slipped from Eurylochus' face at this. The temptation of knowing more than Odysseus was more than he could handle.

"My name is Circe. C-I-R-C-E. This is my island, Aeaea. A-E-A-E-A." She saw me writing which is I guess why she spelled them out. "Come on in. I got sandwiches and snacks and drinks for ya all. And while ya eat, we can talk about getting ya back to Ithaca."

The fact that she'd heard of it made me hopeful that she could help. Also sandwiches and snacks sounded pretty tasty. We all started for the crystal palace. But Circe stopped and put up a hand.

"Nope. No way. No kids," she said.

"But I'm not a kid," I said, even though saying it made me sound like more of a kid.

"Not gonna happen," she said, but then I guess she saw the disappointment on our faces. Or maybe she heard my stomach rumble. "Tell ya what. Ya two little ones just sit on down right out here. I'll have the servants bring ya some sandwiches."

127

"And snacks?" I said.

"And snacks."

So, Dory and I sat on a nearby bench while the guys filed inside.

No sooner were they out of sight, I ran for a window.

"You're not going in," Dory said.

"No. But I'm going to spy on them," I said. "How else will I know what's going on? It's not like Eurylochus is going to give me the truth. Did you hear that? He as good as declared mutiny."

"Yeah, we need to tell Odysseus about that," Dory said, joining me at the window. "That's totally not cool."

The good thing about a palace made of crystal was that even though I couldn't see through it like a window, I could follow shapes and movement. I was able to see where Circe and the guys went, and once they settled down, I found the nearest window and discreetly peeked through.

"I wonder what the best way to cook antelope is," Dory said, watching the herds of animals roaming around.

"You ever cook pork?" I said, looking over at a nearby pen where a couple pink pigs rolled around in the mud. It was a pretty big pigpen. I was surprised Circe didn't have more than two pigs.

"All the time, Homer," Dory said. "Didn't you come by the food truck that time I made those pork dumplings?"

I almost felt the juice running down my chin from the memories. "How could I forget?"

"You know girls have way better memories than guys,"

Dory said.

"That's so not true."

"And hearing," Dory said. "Girls also have way better hearing."

"So, what are they saying in there?" I asked. I wasn't about to admit that she was right, but I couldn't make out a single word.

Dory shook her head. "No clue."

Still, the view was perfect. Circe sat at the head of a long table, and all twenty-two guys sat around. No, scratch that. There were only twenty-one guys. Eurylochus was nowhere to be found.

As we watched, platters of food magically appeared. The men jumped back in surprise, but I guess the magic wasn't enough to compete with their growling tummies. They loaded their plates with sandwiches and chips—even Polites who sat at the opposite end of the table from Circe—and they filled their cups with wine, spilling it over onto the table as they poured. Circe watched them and smiled, motioning for them to take more. They devoured the food.

It was then that I spotted Eurylochus, way off to the side, outside the room, hiding behind a crystal column, peeking in. Maybe he didn't like sandwiches. Not that sailors could be particular about that kind of stuff. Months on a ship had taught me that you eat whatever's put in front of you.

Dory yanked on my sleeve. "Homer."

"What?"

She yanked again. "I thought there were only two pigs."

"There are," I said.

"No. There's a whole bunch."

I zipped my head around to look at the pigpen. Dory was right. It was crammed with pigs now. Pigs of all colors and sizes that dug in the dirt and rolled around on their backs and made cute little pig noises.

Shouts from inside the crystal palace drew my attention back.

The chairs around the table were now empty, all except for where Circe sat at the head of the table. The glasses were overturned. Circe picked the bread off a sandwich and ate the insides.

"Witch! Witch!" Eurylochus shouted and then ran from his hiding spot, dashing from the doorway and through the crystal palace and outside. He didn't stop or look around for us or anything. Instead, he ran back into the woods, toward the ship.

"Do we follow him?" Dory asked, glancing back through the window. Circe, who'd been there only moments before, was gone.

"What about the guys?" I said. "Where are they?" I expected them to run out of the palace at any second, just like Eurylochus, but there was still no sign of them.

"We should look for them," Dory said.

"We should tell Odysseus first."

So, we ran after Eurylochus through the woods to the beach. Eurylochus was just pushing the boat out into the water.

"Where do you think you're going?" Dory said.

"She turned them into swine! Even Pork. She turned them into pigs," Eurylochus said. His eyes were wild and unfocused. He was trying to mess with the oars but not having much success, so Dory and I took over. He babbled the entire time we rowed.

Once we got back to the ship, after a good ten minutes of more nonsense babble, Eurylochus managed to tell Odysseus what had happened.

"She's a witch," Eurylochus said. "We need to leave this place immediately."

But Odysseus shook his head. "Not without my men."

"Your men are pigs," Eurylochus said. "Pork and Polites and Elpenor. And Ear. He was the first. They're all pigs. They're all lost."

"No, they're not," Odysseus said. "We've lost too many already. We aren't going to lose any more."

"Then you're going without me," Eurylochus said.

"Wrong," Odysseus said. "You'll lead me."

Imagine a bunch more back and forth here between the two of them. Suffice it to say that Eurylochus finally gave in. So, we got back into the small boat and rowed to the island. The animals rubbed against us just like before, but now, after seeing what had happened to our guys, I had to wonder if these were animals in the first place. They could be like our guys, humans turned into antelopes and wolves.

Once Eurylochus pointed the way, Odysseus took the lead, pushing through the forest. He held his sword in front of him, ready to strike down the witch. But instead of coming to the garden with the crystal palace, we wound up in a clearing in the middle of the trees. And there, standing in the middle of the clearing, was none other than Hermes himself.

STRANGE BREW

"SEND US BACK!" I SAID, RUNNING FORWARD. THIS was it. Our chance to get back to Ionia. I had the story. I could leave anytime. No matter what Beta said, I didn't need to stick around until Odysseus got home. But Hermes didn't even cast me a second glance.

"Odysseus, man, you are heading into serious danger," Hermes said. "You know that, right?"

"Step aside, god," Odysseus said, puffing out his chest in his pristine yellow tunic. "You can't stop me."

I held up the scroll, trying again. When I got Hermes' attention, I was going to let him know exactly all the thoughts running through my mind. The gods. I can't believe he'd sent us here. We'd been gone forever.

"Did I say I was going to stop you?" Hermes said, turning

his silly winged hat around on his head until it faced backward. The wings, oddly enough, stayed facing forward.

"Some words don't need to be spoken," Odysseus said. "And I'm not willing to lose more men. Now step aside and let us pass."

"You'll fall under her spell," Hermes said. "No one can resist."

Eurylochus stepped forward and put his shoulders back. "I resisted the witch."

"Nope," Hermes said. "She let you go. You were bait."

"I'm not bait."

"Yep. You were supposed to bring Odysseus to her. And look at that. You're doing exactly what she wants you to do."

Confusion clouded Eurylochus' face, but what Hermes said made sense. How else would Eurylochus, who was whiny and annoying and didn't have much to recommend himself, ever get away from Circe?

"What does this witch want with me?" Odysseus said.

"She wants to control you," Hermes said. "That's what Athena says. She knows the witch. And from what Athena says, the witch is crazy." He twirled his finger around his ear in a cuckoo-cuckoo motion.

"Athena is wise," Odysseus said, and his voice got all soft for a second, like it always did when he talked about Athena. "But no one controls me. I've got this. Now step aside."

Great. We were back to the pig-headed Odysseus. Maybe he did deserve to be turned into a swine.

"I guess Athena was right about you," Hermes said.

Odysseus flexed his chest even more than he already was and stood a little taller. "What? That I am brave and strong?"

This made Hermes laugh. "No way. That you're stubborn and arrogant."

"Athena would never say that," Odysseus said.

"Yeah, okay," Hermes said and shook his head. "Never mind. Just take this. It will protect you from the witch."

He plucked a plant from the ground and held it out to Odysseus.

Odysseus narrowed his eyes. "What is it?"

"Holy Moly," Hermes said. "Sure to keep you safe from the powers of the witch."

Odysseus took the plant but studied it suspiciously.

"I want some of that," Eurylochus said.

Hermes shook his head. "No can do. There's only enough for the king."

"But that's not fair," Eurylochus said, reverting back to whining when he didn't get his way.

"If it's true and this witch has turned my men into pigs, how do I turn them back?" Odysseus said.

At this Hermes laughed. "Yeah, that's the hard part. You need to convince Circe to make a deal with you. And deals with Circe … not so easy. She's filled to the top of her head with deception and tricks."

Holy Moly. Witches. Deceptions and tricks. What had we gotten ourselves into this time?

Hermes and Odysseus yammered on for a little bit longer

and figured out exactly how Odysseus would make this deal, and then Odysseus sauntered off, alone. Eurylochus and a couple of the guys who'd come with us went back to the beach to set up camp while they waited for Odysseus to return. I dragged behind.

"What the heck!" I said to Hermes once everyone else except Dory was gone.

"What do you mean, what the heck?" Hermes said.

"You sent us on a crazy, mixed up, completely unsafe journey," I said.

"It's an adventure," Hermes said. "You said you needed an epic story, and I had an epic story that needed a storyteller."

"Yeah," I said. "But we've almost been killed like three times."

"Four times," Dory said.

"Four times," I said.

"But you didn't die, right?" Hermes said.

I balled my hands into fists. "Well, no. But we could have. We definitely could have."

"But you didn't," Hermes said.

"Anyway, we're ready to go back to Ionia now," I said. "Aren't we, Dory?"

She didn't say anything.

"Ready to go back?" Hermes said. "But the story's not over."

He sounded just like Beta.

"It is over," I said, holding up the scroll. "I've gotten tons of good stuff."

Hermes shook his head. "Odysseus isn't home yet. You

can't leave your readers hanging."

My only reader was Elder Pachis, and I was sure that everything I had so far would be enough.

"Just send us back, okay?" I said. "We've been gone for months. How's my mom? Is she okay? Did they take the farm away yet?"

Hermes put up his hands. "The farm is fine. Your mom is okay. But you can't go back yet."

"We have to. These guys are horrible. They're getting into the worst kind of messes, again and again. Just send us home. I know you can do it. You're a god."

Hermes seemed to consider this. "Let's just say you're right. Let's say that I could send you back. What if I didn't want to?"

Blood pounded in my ears. "Didn't want to? Why should you possibly care?"

"Where do you think you are?" Hermes said.

I pressed my hands to the side of my head in frustration. "Some made up fantasy world? A dream? I don't know. I'm just done with it already."

"Of course, you're done with it," Hermes said. "You're living in the past."

I tried to puzzle out what he'd just said, but the blood swooshing around my brain made it really hard to concentrate. "The past? Like time travel?"

Hermes kind of shrugged and nodded at the same time. "Yeah. Like time travel. You went back in time. You guys were only babies when this stuff happened. Everything that's going on now has already happened. But nobody wrote it down. It's why I sent you here. You need to capture this story. You need to make it so people don't forget about it."

The time travel thing noodled around in my brain. "You sent me back in time to write this story for you?"

"You could say that."

"And so what you're saying is that when we get back from our journey—"

"Your adventure," Hermes said.

"Whatever. Our adventure. No time will have passed?"

Hermes put up his hands. "Oh, no. I didn't say that. Did I say that? I didn't mean to say that."

"What exactly did you say?" This was making less sense as the seconds ticked by.

"I sent you ten years in the past to when this whole adventure took place," Hermes said. "Each year that goes by here in the past is a day of your time going by in the future. So if you let all ten days go by ..."

A day for each year. That didn't sound all that bad. And it explained why so little sand had passed through the hourglass. Also, it explained why our hair hadn't grown at all while the guys looked shaggy and scruffy after a week. And no way would it take Odysseus nine more years to get home.

"But," Hermes said, putting up his finger. "I am warning you, so don't say I'm not. If you lose track of time, if all ten years go by, then your farm gets taken away. Your mom gets cast out on the streets. You'll have failed most epically."

"I won't fail," I said.

"I know," Hermes said. "Because I have a solution for that."

"What?" I asked. Ten years seemed like an eternity of time.

"Don't be late," Hermes said, tapping my hourglass. "Keep track of time. Oh, and enjoy the year ahead."

I didn't know what he meant by that. We'd been gone close to a year already. But I didn't get the chance to ask him any more because he flipped his cap back around and vanished.

STANDING ON THE BEACH

THE FIRST THING THAT HAPPENED WAS THAT THE twenty-one guys who'd been turned into pigs came hurrying back to the beach. Pork. Polites. Ear. All of them. Sure, they kept looking back over their shoulder, like they thought Circe was going to snap her fingers and turn them into pigs again, but after a couple glasses of mead, they were fine. The second thing that happened, after he'd calmed down enough, was that Pork said, "The witch says we all get to go hang out at the palace. She promises not to turn us back into anything unnatural."

"Where's Odysseus?" Eurylochus said.

Pork took another huge sip and wiped his mouth with his arm. "I don't think we'll be seeing much of Odysseus anytime soon. The witch has got him. But he says it's okay."

I didn't know what the witch and Odysseus were up to, and

I didn't want to find out.

So, we set up camp in an entire wing of the palace, and we waited. And waited. And waited. And then finally one day—a year had gone by; seriously, a year—Odysseus came sauntering into the room where the guys sat around eating and drinking.

"Are we ready to go yet?" he asked, like he'd only been gone for an hour.

I almost threw a pan at his head, but Dory stopped me. She kind of liked it here because she got to cook and there was all sorts of yummy food, but I was ready to get back on the road. Or the sea, as the case might be.

"Is he kidding?" I muttered under my breath. I'd tried not to panic, but I had to turn the hourglass once already and almost needed to turn it again.

I wasn't the only one ready to leave. Eurylochus stormed forward and got right in Odysseus' face.

"How dare you leave us here for so long?" he said.

"I had no choice," Odysseus said. "To save the men. It was the price I had to pay."

"Save the men," Eurylochus mocked. "We should have left a year ago when we had the chance. We would have been back to Ithaca months ago."

Odysseus pushed him aside, as if to move by. "You don't know what you're talking about, Eurylochus."

"And you don't deserve to be king," Eurylochus said.

The air froze around them. I could not believe he'd just said that. I wrote down every word, trying not to blink so I wouldn't miss anything.

One second went by. Then two. Three. Four. Odysseus' hand went to his sword, but he didn't pull it out. Eurylochus was not so smart. He launched forward and grabbed Odysseus around the neck.

They grappled and fell to the ground. At first the guys cheered them on, most of them rooting for Odysseus. A handful of others calling out Eurylochus' name. He did have some supporters among the guys.

Back and forth they fought, until Odysseus finally landed above Eurylochus. His yellow tunic had been ripped nearly in half. He pulled his sword from its sheath and placed it against Eurylochus' throat.

"What did you say, swine?" Odysseus said.

Eurylochus spotted the cold metal, and his eye grew wide, like somehow he was surprised to see it. But how could he be surprised? Odysseus was the king of Ithaca. Eurylochus was nothing but a wannabe.

"I said that you didn't deserve to be king," Eurylochus said.

I guess he was trying to get himself killed.

"And for that insult, you will die." Odysseus raised the sword and prepared to strike.

"Wait!" Polites said, limping forward.

"Wait for what?" Odysseus said.

"Don't kill him," Polites said. "Not like this."

"His insult is unforgivable," Odysseus said.

I wanted to scream, "Just put down the sword," but I wasn't

about to get in the middle of this fight.

"You can't kill him," Polites said. "It's not what you do."

"He deserves to die," Odysseus said.

Polites shrugged. "I'm not saying I disagree with you. But let the gods be the judge of that. You need to keep your conscience clean."

Odysseus lowered the sword one more time to Eurylochus' neck. And then he did us all proud by hawking up a giant loogie on Eurylochus. It landed right on his eye.

"Only because you're related to my wife am I sparing your life," Odysseus said, and then he stepped back.

We all started breathing again. Then we returned to the ship and got it ready to sail which wasn't an easy task since it had been sitting at the dock for over a year. We patched the leaks with black pitch and mended the blue sail and scrubbed the deck until it shone.

"Where to?" Polites said once everything was ready to go.

Odysseus turned the rudder until it was pointing in the complete opposite direction of Ithaca. "We sail west."

"West?" Eurylochus said. He was right back at it, questioning Odysseus' every move.

"West," Odysseus said. "To edge of the sea. We sail to the Underworld."

It's the Edge of the World as We Know It

As you can imagine, the whole "sail to the Underworld" thing didn't go over so well. The guys questioned and argued and disagreed and even tried reasoning with Odysseus, but—and here's where Odysseus as king really stood out—he had this way of pulling the men toward him. Not of bending their wills, but of convincing them of the beauty of his plan. And by the end of the day, all the guys—well, all except Eurylochus—had the ship ready to sail. They were willing to follow Odysseus, their king, anywhere, even—as Fate would have it—to the Underworld.

"What do you think the Underworld is like?" Dory asked. I sat on my normal bench in the galley and wrote while she made yet another vat of soup. She'd started tucking her hair behind her ears while she worked in the galley, making it even more obvious that she was a girl. But since the guys didn't expect her to be a girl, they still hadn't figured it out. They farted around her and burped so loudly it shook the sails of the ship.

"Dark. Fiery. Depressing," I said. I'd heard stories about the Underworld all my life. Stories that others had told me. Looked like I was the one who'd be telling those stories now.

"That's what I've heard, too," Dory said. "But it can't all be that way? I mean, all the good people go there, too. The guys from the other ships. Your dad. They can't all be burning, can they?"

"My dad's not dead," I said.

"Yeah, okay," Dory replied, but she didn't sound convinced.

"No really," I said. "He's not. He's just taking a long time to get home. Just like Odysseus." This was a good point I made. If Odysseus had been away from his family for years, then there was a really great chance Dad was on his way home also, trying to reach Mom and me. Maybe he'd just run into some Laestrygonians of his own.

"Fine. What about the other guys?" Dory said. "You think it's all fire and brimstone?"

I didn't want to think about Dad dead, and I also didn't want to think about the guys from the ships in some fiery wasteland.

"Probably not," I said.

"But what if it is?" Dory said. "It could be dangerous. We should stay onboard."

"You're kidding, right?"

"No way, Homer," Dory said. "You know that anyone who

goes to the Underworld can never leave again."

"That's just something parents say to scare their kids," I said. "It's not real."

"I wouldn't know," Dory said, and she got real quiet.

I hated that. Dory had no idea who her parents were. They could be ax murderers for all she knew. My dad may be missing, but at least I'd known him. I'd spent the better part of my life with him.

And I missed him.

I wondered if that made it worse, knowing someone and then losing them or not knowing them at all.

"I'm going to the Underworld," I said, holding up the scroll. "It's my job. If I don't write about it then …"

"Then what?" she said.

"Then no one will ever know about it," I said.

"Who cares?" Dory said. "You already have enough. You'll stick with Odysseus for the next couple months until he gets home, and that'll be all you need. You'll pass no problem."

I ran my finger down the smooth scroll. "There's still so much room. So much empty space." Which was actually kind of weird. It seemed like the scroll always made room for more words.

"Some empty space is okay," Dory said. "It helps balance the words."

She was probably right. But I also think that she was scared to go to the Underworld, even if she didn't want to admit it.

Ψ

WE SAILED FOR A MONTH. THE SEA NEVER ENDED. IT didn't seem possible, unless I went with the possibility that we had sailed off the edge of the world and on to some other place. I didn't like this possibility. The idea of leaving the world that I knew behind made my stomach feel all kinds of queasy, like I'd eaten way too much cheese. But unlike eating cheese, which would eventually digest and get better, the tremors in my stomach never stopped. They stayed there as a permanent part of me.

Days blended into nights and then nights blended into days, and then the entire sky went gray and remained that way. Even though I couldn't see it, I had to believe that the sun was still up there somewhere. The guys turned sullen; their moods matched the sky and the water. I wasn't doing much better. I stopped writing when the sky clouded over, and I couldn't bring myself to start again. Dory continued making soup, but it was as bland as everything else.

We didn't speak. None of us had any words we wanted to share.

After the month, a gray harbor appeared before us. The ship drifted up to it, without the guys steering or rowing or anything. Odysseus grabbed from the deck where he'd stored it a jar that Circe had given him and climbed down from the ship onto the long wooden dock that extended into the water.

"Who's with me?" he said. These were the first words anyone had spoken in weeks.

Polites and Eurylochus immediately stepped forward along with five other guys.

I grabbed my scroll from where I'd tucked it away in an oilcloth to keep it safe from the damp air.

"Don't go, Homer," Dory said.

She hadn't forgotten.

"Come with me," I said.

Dory shook her head, and real fear crept into her eyes.

"What are you afraid of?" I asked, grabbing her hand.

"I don't know," she said, and her gaze drifted past me, down the long dock. "I feel like there are secrets out there. Secrets that should maybe remain hidden."

I squeezed her hand. "I'll stay with you the whole time. We'll be together. Everything will be okay."

Dory seemed to consider my words, tossing them back and forth in her mind like coins on a scale.

"But what if it's not okay?" Dory said. "What if …?"

"What if what?" I asked.

She shrugged. "I don't know. Just what if?"

"Then we'll face that what if together," I said. "Now come on. Odysseus is leaving."

Dory finally let me pull her forward, and we hurried down the ladder and caught up with Odysseus and the guys.

He nodded at us. "Bard and Cook. Stay close. There is danger ahead."

Great. His words weren't going to do anything to make Dory feel better.

We walked along the wooden planks into the gray mist until we came to a crack in the world where light seeped through. Odysseus stood tall and sauntered forward, into the crack. The entire world split in half.

The gray mist vanished. We stood on the top of a mountain with brilliant sun shining in the sky above, warming our skin for the first time in a month. A single doorway stood in front of us, surrounded by two columns.

"I go first," Odysseus said, striding forward with the jar in his hands. "Bard, you'll come with me."

Dory stepped forward. "I'll come along, too."

But Odysseus shook his head. "Just the bard." And he shoved me through.

We were no longer on the mountain. The ship and the sea were nowhere to be found. A hard ball formed in my stomach, and I broke out in sweaty chills.

We were in the Underworld.

Two Tickets
for Paradise

AHEAD OF US WAS A RIVER WITH WATER SO BLACK it looked like night had been captured and trapped inside.

"Don't be afraid, Bard," Odysseus said.

"I'm not." I said, but my voice shook, because out of the blackness a boat drifted toward us. It slid up onto the rocky sand where we stood and then a cloaked figure extended a hand, palm up. And I really wished Dory was here next to me, even though she was annoying a lot of the time.

It didn't take a genius to figure out who the cloaked guy was: Charon, Ferryman of the Dead. Everyone knew that Charon was the guy who carted you across the River Styx when it was your time to head to the Underworld. Which it definitely wasn't right now. I had lots of life left ahead of me.

"Did you bring any money?" I whispered to Odysseus. The

only thing in my pockets besides extra ink were crumbs from the rolls Dory snuck me.

"Always be prepared, Bard," Odysseus said, and he reached into his pocket and pulled out two large gold coins.

Two. Which meant that he was planning on me crossing the River Styx along with him.

Odysseus handed the gold coins over to Charon who flipped them around his long bony fingers like some kind of magic trick.

"Good. Good. You brought money," Charon cackled in a voice that sounded like a cross between a crow and a hyena. "So many try to cross without money."

"And do you let them?" I asked, finding my voice even though part of my brain cautioned me to stay really quiet.

Charon leaned way forward until his hood was right in my face. I couldn't see anything inside the hood. It was like an empty pit filled with blackness. But I felt like he could see into my soul.

"Failing school," he said, making a clucking sound. "That's not good at all."

I took a step back. "I'm not failing school."

"You're failing?" Odysseus said. "I was under the assumption that you were a master storyteller."

I put my hands up. "Okay, just a second here. I really don't see how it's either of your business what my grades are."

"It's my business because you're telling my story," Odysseus said.

I crossed my arms. "Then we better get on with that story."

Odysseus laughed, just a small chuckle there by the River Styx, but enough to break through the death around us. "True, Bard. On with our journey."

Charon stepped back to let us by. "Fine. Onto the boat. But don't let your grades slip. School is important, though I don't see being a soldier in your future. No, the Fates have different plans for you."

The Fates had no idea what they were talking about, and neither did Charon. I was definitely going to be a soldier, just like my dad.

"If you take us across, will we be able to come back?" I asked. I had no intention of getting stuck in the Underworld forever.

"Are you dead?" Charon asked.

I shook my head slowly. I may have traveled back in time, thanks to the powers of the gods, but I was not dead. "I'm very much alive. And so is Odysseus."

"Not if he keeps doing stupid stuff," Charon said.

"Stupid like what?" Odysseus said.

"Like making the gods mad," Charon said. "Now get on the boat. Time is wasting."

Odysseus and I climbed aboard. Even though I'd been living on a ship for almost two years, my legs still went all wobbly as the boat swayed in the river. I sank to the bench and leaned out to look over the side as we pulled away from the shore.

"Not too close to the edge," Charon said. "The monsters'll eat something as small as you in one bite."

Monsters. Was there no end to what we'd face? I scooted to the center of the bench, and Charon pushed us across to the other side.

Charon told us not to leave the shore. That the dead would come to us. And then he pushed his black boat back into the black water and slipped away into the fog.

Odysseus sat the giant jug he'd been carting around onto the shore, and we waited, but no dead people showed up. He tried to be all cool, like he had this thing totally under control, but finally he started looking left and right and pacing back and forth.

"She told me to come here. To sacrifice to the dead," Odysseus said. "She told me they would give me guidance."

She had to be Circe. I wasn't about to mention that following the advice of a witch wasn't the smartest thing to do. I figured we could wait a bit longer. Then, when no dead people came to see us, we could leave. Sail back east to Ithaca.

"What's in the jar, anyway?" I asked, bending closer so I could get a better look. It was covered with a thick piece of leather and looked like it had tar inside.

"Our sacrifice," Odysseus said.

"Which is what?" I pulled at the edge of the leather, lifting it just slightly. But maybe I lifted it too much, because a horrendous stench filled the air around us.

"Black blood," Odysseus said.

And the dead began to come.

I recognized the first guy who walked up to us immediately.

It was one of the guys from our ship. I'd just seen him back on Circe's island.

"Elpenor!" Odysseus said. "What are you doing here?"

It was obvious that he was being dead here. He didn't act like he recognized us at all. Instead, he drifted forward, sniffing the air, until he was right in front of the jar of black blood. Without a word, he lifted the jar to his mouth and drank. His lips were covered in the blood, but he licked them clean and recognition finally registered in his eyes.

"King Odysseus, you left me," he said.

"Left you?" Odysseus said. "We stayed for a year. Then we sailed on. Why weren't you on the ship when we set sail?"

Come to think of it, I hadn't seen this guy since before we left the island.

"I fell off a roof, man," Elpenor said. "Nobody noticed."

"Fell off a roof?" Odysseus said. "Why in the name of the gods would you do that?"

"I didn't mean to," Elpenor said. "It was an accident. I had way too much of that mead. And now all these animals are grazing around my body, peeing on me. Maybe, if it's not too much trouble, you could come back and bury me."

Everyone knew you had to bury the dead. Otherwise they'd never be at rest. It was just one of those things taught since birth. Respected.

"Consider it done," Odysseus said because this was his crewmate. "We will give you the rest you deserve."

"Thank you," Elpenor said.

"Oh, and sorry that nobody noticed," I added. That seemed like the worst part of it. That this poor guy had gone and fallen off the roof and died and nobody had even noticed he was gone. I liked to think that Dory, at least, had my back should I ever fall off a roof and die.

"It's good to have friends," Elpenor said, and then he walked away.

Some old guy walked up to us next. No wait. It was a lady. No, that wasn't right. It was a guy, but he looked a lot like a woman with his long hair as the lights around the shore shone down on him. He didn't even look at the jar of blood.

"King Odysseus," the old guy said.

"Prophet Tiresias," Odysseus said, and he bowed low.

"Prophet!" the old guy said. "That's a hoot! I haven't told a prophecy in years."

This wasn't sounding all that encouraging.

"We come for your help," Odysseus said.

"Help! What help can I offer the King of Ithaca?" Tiresias said.

"Well, man, that's the problem," Odysseus said. "We're having a bit of an issue getting back." And Odysseus told him all about the cyclops and our fight with Poseidon, and how now Poseidon was making it super hard for us to get home.

"You messed up, Odysseus," Tiresias said. "You shouldn't have made the god angry in the first place."

Odysseus pursed his lips. "Be that as it may be, the damage is done. What can I do about it now?"

"Not much," Tiresias said. "Except try to make it up to the god."

"And how should I do that?" Odysseus said. "I seek your guidance."

Tiresias pulled a rolled-up scroll out from under his robes. "I've got a twelve step plan for you, including what you should do once you get back to Ithaca," he said, handing it over. "But I'm going to warn you. It's not easy. The first step is the hardest. You have to admit that you're powerless in the face of the gods."

Odysseus studied the list, and his eyes narrowed with each line he read.

"Hmmm …," Odysseus said. "These steps will not be easy."

Nothing on this journey had been easy so far. I didn't see how Odysseus thought anything was going to change.

"But if this is what it takes, then I will make it my master," Odysseus said, stuffing the list into his pocket.

"Oh, and one more thing," Tiresias said. "Don't eat the cattle."

"What cattle?" Odysseus asked, but Tiresias faded away.

"So, we got what we came for?" I said.

"Possibly," Odysseus said, but then another person appeared on the shore and walked over to the jar.

"Mother," Odysseus said when he saw her.

Recognition didn't shine in her eyes until she finished drinking from the jar of blood. But then, she saw her son, and she ran to him, and they embraced. And tears ran down Odysseus' face.

156

"What evil is this that you are here, Mother?" Odysseus said.

She pulled back from the hug, and then she slapped him. "You left your poor mother," she said. "What kind of son are you? For years on end. I watched out for your wife and your son, but you stayed away so long."

"It's taken us longer to return than I had hoped," Odysseus said. "But we're coming. I swear it."

"And what do you swear on? Your mother's grave? Because that's what you'll find when you get back there."

"But why did you die? How did this horror come to be?"

Well, it turned out that his mom died from being so sad because he'd been gone so long. And then she filled him in on everything that he'd been missing at home. And the more words she spoke, the angrier Odysseus grew.

"Poseidon will pay for keeping me away for so long," Odysseus said.

"No," I piped up before I thought better of it. "Don't you get it? You need to make up with Poseidon. Not make him even angrier."

"The boy is right," Odysseus' mom said, thumping him on the side of the head. "Use that brain of yours. You're not king for nothing."

She faded away. But my mind started churning. And my heart pounded in my chest.

A couple other guys visited Odysseus after his mom. Agamemnon, who'd been the king who convinced Odysseus to fight in the war in the first place. Odysseus hadn't known he was dead. Achilles, this awesome hero from the Trojan War who the guys talked about like he was some sort of god. I couldn't focus on either of them. Now that Odysseus had seen his mom, my mind could only think of one thing.

Because I had to know. One way or the other.

I closed my eyes and prayed to see him if he was here. I prayed to Hermes because he kind of seemed like he was on my side. I prayed to Hades and Persephone since they ruled the Underworld. And then I just prayed. To any god who might listen and grant me this one small request.

And then I prayed that he didn't show up. That he really was still alive and my hope that I'd been holding onto for so long wasn't in vain.

But it wasn't to be.

From the darkness, a shadow appeared. Odysseus, as if he knew, took a step back. The shadow crept to the jar of blood and drank. And then his eyes found mine and recognition brightened his face.

"Homer!" he called and held his arms open wide.

My heart sank because seeing him here meant he really was dead. He wasn't on a journey to come home to Mom and me. We'd never see him again, at least not outside of this place. And the sorrow of this thought threatened to overwhelm me. But the happiness on Dad's face forced me to push past it. If this was the only chance I had to see Dad—to get the closure that I desperately needed—then I was not going to waste it.

"Dad!" I said, and I ran toward him and let him engulf

me in his arms, just like he'd done so many times when I was younger. He held me tight and stroked my hair, and I pressed my face against his chest and wished that I could stay here forever, with him.

"Homer, look at you," Dad said, stepping back enough that he could see me. "You're so grown up. What happened?"

"Puberty?" I said, trying to use humor to avoid the true crushing emotions that ran through me.

"Has it been that long?" Dad asked.

"Over two years," I said. "I waited for you. I turned the hourglass just like you told me to. I went to town when the other soldiers came home. But you weren't there. You never came back."

"And I'm so sorry," Dad said. "I thought about you every day. Missed you so much. I used to tell stories about you. To the other soldiers. Did you know that?"

I shook my head, not trusting myself to speak.

"I told them how brave you were. And how smart you were. And how I knew you were destined for great things."

I swallowed hard, not wanting to disappoint Dad by telling him how wrong he was.

Dad laughed and ruffled my hair. "It does my heart good to see you so grown up."

"It does my heart good to see you," I said and swallowed the lump in my throat.

"How is your mother?" Dad asked. "Are you taking care of her, now that you're head of the household?"

I thought about how close I'd come to failing so many times already. And how if I failed, Mom would be lost. And how I had to tell her that Dad really was dead. That he wasn't coming back. Every bit of determination inside me doubled. I had to get home. I could not fail Mom, and I could not let Dad down.

"I'm taking really good care of her, Dad," I said. "But she misses you. We both do."

He reached forward and grasped the hourglass hanging around my neck. "I'm always with you, Homer. Even when you think I'm not. I'm there, watching you. Just talk to me, if you need to. I'll hear you, even if I can't answer. I'll be there beside you. Always."

I wrapped my hands around his, realizing how small my hands were in comparison to him. I still had a lot of growing to do before I became anywhere near the man that Dad was.

"I love you, Dad," I said.

"I love you, Homer." And with that, Dad drifted away.

As if he knew exactly what I needed, Odysseus stepped forward and rested his hand on my shoulder.

"He would be proud of you, Bard," Odysseus said. "Your bravery. Your loyalty. Your determination. Just as I'm proud of you. The world needs people like you. People who make a difference."

I nodded slowly. I had to stay the path. Continue to make him proud. Make them both proud.

Odysseus and I stayed there until the silhouette of Dad slipped back into shadow and vanished entirely. And then the rustling of the dead began again.

One more person came toward us. He drank from the jar of blood, and recognition registered in his eyes.

"Ajax," Odysseus said, and he moved forward to greet the dead.

But Ajax turned his back and refused to talk to Odysseus, no matter what Odysseus said.

So finally, Odysseus gave up. It was one conversation that was not meant to be.

We turned back to the water. The boat with Charon was just coming to shore. And there, right up front, was Dory.

Dory got off the boat even as Odysseus stepped on.

"What are you doing here?" I asked.

"I had to come," Dory said, and then her eyes drifted past me to the figure who still stood on the beach with his back toward us.

She walked forward, toward Ajax. I trailed after her because I didn't like the idea of her going ahead alone. And when she got about five feet away from the dead Greek hero, he turned to face her.

"You're alive," Ajax said when his eyes found her.

Dory nodded slowly. "You called me here," she said. "In my mind. I heard you. But do I know you?"

"I thought you were dead," Ajax said. "I thought they killed you. You were just a baby."

Wait. I had no clue what was going on here. Ajax knew who Dory was? But how was that even possible? Dory was from

Ionia. A slave. Ajax had been in Troy, fighting in the war.

"I remember … noise," Dory said. "Fear."

"I thought I'd never see you again," Ajax said. "You were supposed to be on a ship. I put you there myself. But then the ship … They said it was destroyed."

"I don't know you," Dory said, but she didn't sound entirely convinced.

"I know you," Ajax said. "And I'm sorry I failed you." Then a single tear rolled down his face before he turned away. And that's when I noticed that the tattoo Dory had on the back of her neck that she always tried to keep hidden … Ajax had one just like it. And I knew I'd seen the tattooed symbol somewhere else—it was really familiar—but I couldn't remember where.

We waited until Ajax faded into the mist, then we turned and walked away, back to the boat where Odysseus and Charon waited. Odysseus didn't ask Dory what Ajax had said, and she didn't offer it up either. We drifted across the River Styx and through the crack in the world and back to where the guys waited.

Odysseus didn't talk about what had happened in the Underworld. But I wrote it all down because it was definitely a part of his story. The part with Dad wasn't. I kept that to myself. I'd share it with Mom once I got home. Because I would get home.

As for the conversation with Ajax, I wrote that down, too. And I drew the symbol. The tattoo. It might not fit in the same story as Odysseus, but it must have a story all of its own.

Same Song, Second Verse

WE STOPPED BACK BY TO VISIT CIRCE. YOU'D THINK that after a year on her island, the guys would have been used to her by now, but they still crept around her like they were scared she'd turn them into farm animals again.

She didn't.

We buried Elpenor. His body was right where he'd said it was. Once the guys found out he was dead, they all felt guilty, and so his eulogy went on for two days because they all wanted a chance to talk about what a great guy he was. Pretty sure he would have chuckled at that since they hadn't noticed he was gone, but it made for a nice funeral. Of course, then they all celebrated some more and drank a bunch of mead, which took another week.

Circe spent more time with Odysseus, giving him a bunch

163

of advice that I hoped would keep us from getting killed. We couldn't stand to lose anyone else. And then finally we left the island.

"Prettiest witch I've ever seen," Odysseus said, straightening his fresh yellow tunic.

I didn't think his wife, Penelope, would be too happy about that comment.

The final sands in the tiny hourglass fell through to the bottom, and I flipped it. My third rotation. But I wasn't worried. I still had plenty of time.

"Have you thought any more about it?" I asked Dory as the guys rowed the ship away from Circe's island.

"About what Ajax said?" she asked.

I nodded.

"Some," she said. "But I still don't remember much."

I'd thought a lot about Dad. And sure, I wished he weren't dead, that he were back at home waiting for me, but at least I knew now.

"He had the same tattoo as you," I said.

Immediately her hand went to the back of her neck. "You've seen it?"

"Of course, I've seen it," I said. "We've been around each other twenty-four/seven for the last two years."

"You weren't supposed to see it," she said.

"Why? What is it?"

Dory shook her head. "I don't know. I've always had it. Always kept it hidden. I guess I've just always has this feeling like I'm supposed to keep it secret."

"But why does Ajax have it, too?"

"No clue," Dory said. "Just promise me you won't tell anyone."

"I won't tell anyone," I said. "I can keep your secrets."

"What secrets?" Eurylochus said, sneaking into the galley like the rat that he was.

"No secrets," I said quickly. Too quickly.

Eurylochus strolled forward and got right in Dory's face. "Cook, I know you're keeping secrets. And I'll find out what they are. And if for some reason I find out that you're responsible for our not reaching Ithaca, I'll have you thrown overboard."

I shoved my way in between them. "Dory isn't responsible for us not reaching Ithaca," I said. "That's ridiculous."

Eurylochus narrowed his eyes. "Just know that I'm watching you always. One slip, and you're shark fodder."

He shoved me backward and left the room.

"That guy's like a wet sock," Dory said, trying to diffuse the tension in the air.

"Or an itchy sweater," I added. "There's nothing worse than an itchy sweater."

"Except a wet sock."

"What'd you do to make him so mad?" I asked. My heart pounded. There was no possible way he knew Dory was a girl.

Dory shrugged. "Maybe he doesn't like the soup?"

Maybe. Or maybe there was something else. All I knew was that Dory had to be extra careful.

Ψ

ONCE WE'D SAILED FOR A FEW DAYS, ODYSSEUS came into the galley.

"Cook, do we have any beeswax?" he said.

"Possibly," Dory said, standing protectively in front of the supply cabinets. She hated how just since he was king, he thought he should get whatever he wanted whenever he wanted.

"I'll be needing it," he said.

"Why?" Dory asked.

"Why do you always question me?" Odysseus said. "I'm the king."

"Not my king," Dory said, and I kind of cringed at her words. She'd gotten a bit more outspoken since our visit to the Underworld.

"Just give me the beeswax, Cook," Odysseus said.

"Fine," she said, handing it over. "But bring me back what you don't use."

I followed Odysseus up to the deck to see what crazy scheme he had going on this time. In addition to the jar full of wax, a bunch of rope lay coiled on the deck.

"You want us to do what?" Eurylochus said.

"I want you to tie me to the mast," Odysseus said. "And then I want you all to stuff wax in your ears."

"And why is that, great king?" Eurylochus said. He never gave up on pushing Odysseus' buttons.

"Because I want to save your lives," Odysseus said.

The guys laughed.

"Save our lives from what?" a guy we called Skinner said. He wore a tunic made of eel skins, hence the nickname.

"Killer mermaids," Odysseus said, which was completely the wrong thing to say. Killer mermaids. I could almost imagine mermaids with long fangs jumping at the guys and sucking the blood from their bodies.

"Mermaids are no match for us," Eurylochus said, and a bunch of the guys cheered and held up their swords, like they were ready to fight anything put in front of them.

"These are not just mermaids," Polites said, leaning forward. "I've heard stories of these creatures that haunt the sea."

"What kind of stories?" another guy said. He'd spent a lot of the year on Circe's island patching the men's clothes, so everyone called him Tailor. He was also the one who made sure Odysseus' yellow tunic looked brand new no matter how many time he ripped it.

"Stories about what they will do to men if they catch them," Polites said.

"And what's that?" Skinner said. But he said it with a stupid smile on his face, like he thought the killer mermaids were going to bring them milk and cookies instead of sucking them dry.

"They devour them, bit by bit," Polites said. "One finger after another. They take their time. And the entire time, while they do this, they sing a song."

"A song!" I said. "I know what you're talking about."

Polites looked at me and raised his visible eyebrow, inviting me to tell more. So I did. I leaned my elbows back on the deck and told the guys what I knew.

"They're the Sirens," I said. "I learned about them in school. They wait by the water, sitting on the rocks. And when ships sail by, they sing to the men."

"Music doesn't sound so bad," Tailor said. "Sometimes it helps me concentrate."

I shook my head. "This is how they draw victims. They sing to them, such amazing music—and no, before you guys ask, I don't know what it sounds like. But they sing it, and men become hypnotized. They jump into the water, and that's when the sirens attack."

"So they are killer mermaids," Skinner said.

"Yeah," I said. "But they weren't always. Rumors have it that they used to be best friends with Persephone."

"I love Persephone," Pork said. "Like if I could meet a goddess, that's who it would be. Anyone who can put up with Hades and the Underworld has to be pretty hot."

"No pun intended," Dory said.

I'm not sure half the guys got the joke, but they all laughed.

"So, they were her best friends, and they were there when Hades took Persephone away," I said. "And what I learned was that her mom, Demeter, was so mad at them that she turned them into monsters."

"Pretty monsters who sing," Tailor said. He still didn't get it.

"Seems kind of unfair of Demeter," Dory said.

I'd thought the same thing when I heard the story, back in school, but I kept my mouth shut. I wasn't going to get another god or goddess mad at us. But I couldn't believe that I remembered the story. It was like now that I thought about it, I'd actually learned a lot more than I realized I had. Elder Pachis would be impressed … if I ever made it home.

"Enough talk, men," Odysseus said. "We will be reaching the waters of the Sirens very soon."

So, we went with his plan. The guys tied Odysseus to the mast, making sure to double and triple knot all the ropes. Then, they stuffed wax in their ears.

"Tie me up," I said to Dory, handing her a giant coil of rope.

"No way, Homer," she said, and she handed me some wax.

I balled the wax in my fist. "Yes, way. I'm supposed to be writing this story. And if I have my ears plugged, I won't know what's going on. So, you have to tie me up."

"I'll tell you later," she said.

I shook my head. "No way. You need to plug your ears."

"No, Homer. I don't."

"Don't be stupid. Of course you do. Did you not hear the part about them making men jump to their death?" I said.

"I heard it perfectly," Dory said. "The Sirens make 'the men' jump to their death."

Oh. Yeah. That was true.

"Okay, fine. Then just tie me up and pretend to tie yourself up, too, just in case the guys are watching."

So that's what we did. Dory tied me to a mast near the back

of the boat. She made sure the ropes were extra tight. Probably tighter than they needed to be. And then she tied herself next to me, looping the rope loosely around her waist and hands.

Then we waited.

SIREN'S SONG

THE MUSIC BEGAN LIKE A WHISPER ON THE WAVES . . .

"I like that," Dory said. "It sounds so poetic."

"Thanks. I'm still working on the Dactylic Hexameter part of it," I said, and I went back to my writing.

The music began like a whisper on the waves, so faint I almost thought it was the wind. But as we sailed closer to the island, a melody formed and reached my ears. I was immediately filled with the deepest contentment I'd ever felt in my life. Like I knew, more than anything in the world, that everything was going to be okay. Dad. Mom. Odysseus. Everything would work out.

The guys didn't even acknowledge the song. They went on about their sailing duties, doing things like making sure the ship didn't smash against the rocks and other important stuff like that. As for Odysseus, his face looked exactly how I felt. Like he'd found eternal bliss.

"Do you hear it?" Dory said.

I felt like I should answer, but I couldn't bring myself to open my mouth and speak to her. All that mattered was listening to the music.

Words formed among the melody. And with the words was the promise of knowledge like I had never imagined possible. If I went with the Sirens, I would know the past. I would see the future. I would contain every bit of knowledge in the universe. I could predict what would happen, well before it happened. Others would come to me for guidance. I would be a scholar beyond all others. Elder Pachis would bow down to me because my knowledge would be so great.

From the center mast, Odysseus started crying. He begged the men to release him. I knew this is what he was doing, because I was doing the same. All I wanted, more than anything in the world, was access to that knowledge. The knowledge would set me free. It would pave the way for my life ahead.

"Please let me loose," I begged Dory.

I don't know if she heard. None of the guys did. And I stayed tied to the mast like that, even as the Siren song continued.

If Dory wasn't going to let me go, then I would have to find a way to free myself. I started moving my hands up and down, scraping the rope against the wood of the deck. Splinters dug into my wrists, but I didn't care. I had to get free. The ropes were tight, but I made progress, and soon I could move them six inches. Then nearly a foot. A couple more seconds and I would escape.

Except then Polites saw what I was doing and ran over to the mast where we were tied. He didn't say a word, only bound new ropes around my wrists, even as I said horrible things to him, telling him what an awful person he was for not freeing me. I guess he couldn't hear, seeing as how he had the wax stuffed in his ears. And then, once he'd finished binding me, he crossed his arms and positioned himself over me and waited.

The song continued, even as the island of the Sirens slipped away. And just before their song was out of reach, their final words came, just for me.

"Look to the seal, Homer," one sang. *"Look to the seal."*

"The seal is the answer," another sang. *"The seal is the answer."*

"The seal will set her free," the third sang. *"Set her free."*

I clutched toward their words trying to hold on to them, but it was no use. We were too far. As their song drifted farther and farther away, I mapped out my plan. Once Dory and Polites cut me free, I would jump from the deck and swim back to the Sirens. They would give me the knowledge. And everything would be exactly as it should be.

The sun crossed the sky, dipping toward the horizon behind us as the hours passed. The melody continued, but also faded, like the setting sun. And only when it dipped halfway below the sea, did Polites finally release me. I fell to the deck and lay curled in a ball, processing the bits of knowledge the Sirens had given. Or at least I tried to process them. When I searched my memories, they kept slipping away, almost like pieces of a dream. And I couldn't for the life of me imagine what they'd said being so important.

"Do you remember the song?" I asked Dory. Polites was back over by Odysseus cutting the ropes that bound him. Once free, he fell to the deck, just like I had.

Dory leaned close and whispered. "There was no song, Homer."

"There was. Maybe you just couldn't hear it."

Dory put her hands on her hips. "Oh, really. What did they say?"

I shook my head. "I don't remember. But it was there. It was ... beautiful. And there was something about a ..."

"A what?" Dory asked.

"A ..." I tried to remember. I really did. But it seemed like the more I thought about it, the more it slipped out of my mind.

"Yeah, well if you remember, let me know."

I looked around the deck, at the guys running from one side to the next, getting the ship ready for nightfall.

"Everyone's alive?" I asked Polites once he came back over to join us.

"Every single one," he said. "But Odysseus says—"

"The worst is ahead," Odysseus finished, walking up right then.

"What do you mean, the worst is ahead?" I said. "You keep saying that. All the time. And I keep writing, recording the story. How can the worst be ahead? When are we going to get to Ithaca?"

My voice was raised, but I didn't care. This was getting flat out ridiculous. A witch. The Underworld. Sirens. What could possibly be next?

Odysseus' eyes softened. "I understand, Bard. A journey like this isn't easy for any of us. And not all will stay the course. That makes the story even harder. But I promise you. We will get to Ithaca."

I wasn't sure how he could be so sure. To me, it seemed like we were going from one death trap to the next.

"We stay this course for the remainder of the week," Odysseus said. "We rest when we can. Because that is when the worst will come."

Nothing was worse than everything we'd already been through. But whatever. That meant I had a week to catch up on the story. I'd write down everything I could remember about the Sirens. Maybe what they said would come back to me. Or maybe I was better off forgetting.

Don't Stop Believing

The day started out bad and got worse. Dory came up onto deck and told Odysseus we only had enough food for two more days. This didn't make the men too happy.

Okay, fine, I didn't want to mention it, but they started kicking things around the deck and throwing temper tantrums like two-year-olds. Not that I remember throwing tantrums when I was two. Mom always said I did, but I'm not sure that I believe her.

"Anyway, get on with the story, Homer," Dory said.

Right. On with the story.

So, the guys were all upset. And Odysseus told them to cool it or he'd throw them overboard.

No, he wouldn't really have thrown them overboard.

Wait, they did throw the old cook overboard before we'd

come along.

"Anyway …"

Anyway, once he finally got them to settle down, Odysseus called a meeting. Yeah, meetings were not good. This meant the something bad that we'd been waiting for was getting close.

"Rocks ahead," Polites called from the crow's nest.

"And that's what I want to talk to you all about," Odysseus said. Then, he told us about the two monsters, because hey, one monster is never enough.

"You can't have two monsters," Dory said, shaking her head.

"What do you mean, I can't have two monsters?" I asked as I scribbled down the story.

"I mean you can't have two monsters," Dory said. "It's too much." She put her hands on her hips like she always did when she lectured me. "You might get your readers to believe in one monster. But when you start throwing two monsters at them, they can't handle it. They'll stop believing."

I scribbled, *"Don't stop believing,"* in the margin, next to the text. I didn't want people to lose faith.

"I didn't make up the story," I said. And I went on writing, and Odysseus went on talking. He loved to hear himself speak.

"The first is called Scylla," Odysseus said.

"I've heard stories of Scylla," Eurylochus said. "She's not all that scary."

I'll give Odysseus credit. He didn't even acknowledge the comment.

"According to Circe …," Odysseus started, but man,

177

sometimes his stories could be so dry. He used all these big words that had nothing to do with the information he was trying to give. I figured he just thought they made him sound smarter.

So I'll summarize.

There used to be this really hot girl named Scylla. Her mom was an equally hot sea nymph which is also pretty cool. Anyway, one day, get this, the girl made the gods mad. And if we've all learned one thing so far on this fun little adventure, it's not to make the gods angry. But she did. And, of course, they turned her into a heinous monster, because that's what happens when you make the gods mad.

So yeah, now she's a monster. She lives on a rock. And she eats people. But—and here's the fun part—she has six heads, so she doesn't eat just one person. She eats six. Every time she pounces.

"So, if she pounced four times, she'd eat twenty-four of us," Dory said. She loved the whole math thing and measured out ingredients when there was nothing else to do.

"Yeah, twenty-four."

"And if she pounces five times," Dory said. "Then we're up to thirty."

I put up my hand. "Wait. There's a way to keep her from pouncing more than once."

"Great," Dory said. "What? Do we throw half the men overboard?"

I shook my head. "Nothing like that. We have to pray to her mom. You remember, the hot sea nymph."

"Do you have to say 'hot'?" Dory said. "It's so degrading."

"What should I say?"

"Really good looking?" she suggested.

"Fine. Whatever. We pray to the really good looking sea nymph and ask her to ask her daughter to only pounce once."

"Great. So only six of us die," Dory said. "How encouraging."

That's when Odysseus started telling us about the other monster.

"As for the other monster …"

I summarized again.

"Charybdis," I said. "Nobody knows what she looks like."

"She?" Dory said. "If nobody knows what she looks like, how do you know she's a girl?"

I shrugged. "Because rumor has it that she's the daughter of Poseidon."

"The god who hates us," Dory said.

"Yep," I said. "And that would be a problem. Sure, she lives under the water. But, before you think we can just slip by, un-noticed, get this. Three times a day, Charybdis swallows a huge amount of water and then spits it back out, making whirlpools that can engulf ships whole."

"So, we just go past it not during those three times," Eurylochus said. He smiled like he'd just solved the Pythagorean Theorem.

"And what times are those?" Odysseus said, finally ac-knowledging the snot of a man.

"You're the leader," Eurylochus said. "You tell us. What did the witch say?"

"Circe," Odysseus said, emphasizing her name, "said that the monster was completely unpredictable. That we would be much better off steering as close to Scylla as possible."

"And have six of us get eaten?" Pork said. "I don't like that." He did have a point.

"Better six than our entire ship," Odysseus said.

He had a point, too.

And because Odysseus was the king, we went with his plan. Here's how it all went down.

"I need the rowers to their oars," Odysseus said.

You've never seen guys move so fast. They dashed to the benches, all trying to get the farthest spot away from the edge of the boat. The fact that they were sitting low on the deck had to be an advantage.

Next Odysseus had the rest of the guys lower and angle the masts so we'd veer toward the north, where Scylla lived, not the south where Charybdis waited. He then asked for volunteers to pray to Scylla's mom. Ten guys offered. Odysseus sent them to the front of the ship so their prayers would be closest to our impending doom. They dropped to their knees and prayed.

And then the drum started, and the ship launched forward.

"You should go below deck," I said to Dory.

"Are you kidding me, Homer?" she said.

"No, I'm not kidding," I said. "This is real. You could die."

"Like the ten other times I could have died but didn't," she said.

"Still, I hate the idea of you up here."

"Why? Because I'm a girl?" she whisper-hissed. But she said it way too loud.

"What was that?" Eurylochus said, spinning to face us.

Crud.

"Nothing," I said.

"It sounded like—" Eurylochus began.

"We're working on the story," I said, holding up the scroll. The guys—even Eurylochus—knew to respect the scroll.

He narrowed his eyes. "I suggest you work on it under the deck. Danger is ahead." Then he headed to the back of the ship to stand by Polites and Odysseus.

I knew one thing. I wasn't leaving. If I got all my story info secondhand, it wasn't going to be worth squat.

"You need to be a little quieter," I whispered to Dory. "Are you seriously trying to get the guys to throw you overboard? Because I'm pretty sure they will if they think it will help them get around these monsters."

Dory rolled her eyes. "Being a girl has nothing to do with all the problems we've had. That's totally on Odysseus. If he wasn't such an arrogant idiot, none of this would have happened."

She was right, but I didn't think the guys would see it that way, especially if they thought it improved their odds of staying alive.

We pulled forward, and when I saw what was ahead, my stomach got this awful feeling in it, like I'd eaten way too much greasy falafel. We were all going to die.

No, that wasn't going to happen. I had to get this story back to Elder Pachis. If I didn't, Mom would lose not only Dad but me. I couldn't let that happen. I couldn't disappoint her.

I rolled the scroll and tucked it inside my shirt and then stuffed the pen and ink in my pockets. I was not going to live through certain doom only to lose the story that I'd worked so hard to collect.

The guys were tense, pulling on the ropes and holding onto the railing. None of them wanted to get eaten. And maybe, if their prayers were strong enough, none of them would. Scylla could take mercy on us and let us pass, untouched.

Dory walked to the edge of the railing, near the front of the ship.

I ran after her. "What are you doing?"

She tossed her head back and faced forward. "I'm not going to let the monsters scare me."

"Are you stupid?" I said. "The monsters are scary. They should scare you."

"I'm not afraid of them," she said.

Was she kidding? She had to be, because in front of us was certain death like I'd never seen before. Huge rocks rose out of the water on either side of a tiny little passageway. It was hardly big enough for the boat to pass through unharmed even if there weren't any monsters. The rocks looked like they had pointed spikes. If the ship hit them, that would be just one more way for us all to die.

On the right, the water swirled and spun, spewing huge

clouds of mist and water, like a tornado both sucking water down and spitting it back up. That was Charybdis. Fully active. There was no changing our minds now. We were going too fast. If we got near her, she'd drown us all.

On the left, the water sat calm. Way too calm. And the rocks … There was nothing on them. Just spiky, scary rocks, but no Scylla.

Odysseus put a finger to his lips, like maybe we could slip by unnoticed. Or maybe Scylla had gone away. Decided not to mess with us.

"Where is she?" Dory whispered. Even though she was trying to act all brave, her fingers had turned white from where she clutched the railing. Mine had too. But I was fine with admitting that the holy crap was scared out of me.

"I don't know," I whispered back.

We continued forward, and Odysseus steered us closer to the empty shore, as far away from Charybdis as we could possibly get. Every single one of the guys had the same expression. It was a weird mix of confusion and fear and hope. Hope that Scylla was not there. And they were silent. As quiet as when we'd passed into the Underworld. The only sound was the swirling water of the whirlpool off to our right.

I reached over and grabbed Dory's hand, and she didn't pull away. And we waited as our ship closed in.

The bow of the ship reached the rocks and continued on. Still no Scylla. The men rowed, averting their eyes from the rocks, like maybe if they didn't see any problems, there wouldn't be any. I knew how they felt. It was like walking through a dark room, worrying about monsters under the bed.

Onward the ship went, plowing through the water. We were halfway past. The rocks were quiet. Empty. I held my breath without realizing it. I didn't want to risk making a single sound. Some of the guys' mouths moved in silent prayer, still praying to Scylla's mom for our lives.

The ship was nearly through. The wind picked up, gently rustling over the rocks. Odysseus watched the shore the same as I did. Please let us get past. Just this once.

But the wind made a horrible hissing sound, and out of a cave hidden in the rocks, the monster appeared. She flew up from her hiding place, six heads, six hungry mouths.

"Row, men!" Odysseus shouted.

She pounced, and each of her heads grabbed one of the guys. Some were rowers. Some were manning the sails. She wasn't selective. And then, with the guys in her mouths, she vanished back into her terrible hiding place.

THE SAD PARTS

I KNEW THESE GUYS. EAR. THE GUY WHO HANGS out with Fish. Lefty. I liked these guys. And I didn't want to think about them gone. But no matter how much I might have wanted to change what had just happened, there was no going back. Six of the guys were gone. And we were free from the monsters.

Dory stared back at the rocky shore, like she was still trying to process what had happened.

"How do you write about that, Homer?" she asked.

I hadn't gotten my scroll and pen out yet. I couldn't. It was too soon. Too raw.

I shook my head. "I don't know. I think … that maybe there are times when we're telling stories and bad things happen. And even if the story might be about adventure and Odysseus getting home, we have to talk about those bad things, too."

"But they're sad," she said, and she wiped a tear.

I'd never seen Dory cry, but I didn't mention it. I only wiped away my own tears. And our ship sailed forward, on toward Ithaca.

WARNINGS OF THE DEAD

IT WAS WAY LATE IN THE DAY WHEN THE SILENCE that had smothered our ship finally lifted.

"Cook, how goes dinner?" Odysseus asked.

Dory glared at him. "How can you think about food at a time like this?"

Odysseus glanced over his shoulder and then turned back to us. "Because if I don't think about food, then the men will begin to think about food, and if they find no food, then their already tense attitudes will shatter. Do you want their attitudes to shatter?"

Another point for Odysseus. Another reason he was king. He was right. He had to think about these things ahead of time.

"Come on," I said, grabbing Dory's arm. "I'll help you get dinner ready."

She nodded without a word, and we headed below deck. I'd spent the better part of the day writing in silence. It amazed me how much I could get done with no distractions. No guys shouting. No singing. Just me and my story.

"You realize we're back to our original problem," Dory said.

"What problem?" I asked. Best I could remember, we'd left our problems behind when we passed by the two monsters.

She held up an empty soup pot. "Food. We're low on food."

Oh yeah. That was how the day started. And here we were, a horrible eight hours later, and that's how it was ending.

"Do you have enough to make anything for at least a few days?" I asked. "Odysseus says we'll be back to Ithaca by then."

Dory erupted in a burst of laughter. "And you believe him?"

"Shhh …," I said, but she didn't stop laughing. And pretty soon, I started laughing, too, because the entire thing was so ridiculous. We should have been to Ithaca over two years ago.

We laughed until we cried, and then we laughed more. Tears streamed down our faces from all the emotions being released.

"It doesn't seem like you two are making dinner," Polites said, coming into the galley.

I clutched at my belly. It hurt from the exertion of the laughter.

"We're working on it," Dory said, but she giggled again.

Polites just shook his head. "Don't let Odysseus see you."

And then he helped us figure out how we could make the remaining food stretch for a couple days. But that was going to be it. If we didn't get to Ithaca tomorrow, we were going to have to start fishing again.

Ψ

WE DIDN'T SEE ANY LAND THE NEXT DAY. OR THE next. Or for a week. So much for Ithaca. But after nearly two weeks went by, Polites spotted an island.

"Ahead!" he called and pointed to the south.

Every head on deck swiveled to look. And there it was. A gem of an island brilliant and green and shining like the sun was casting down light just for it.

Odysseus barreled to the middle of the deck and put up his hands. "We can't stop there, men."

Yeah, you can imagine how well this went over. Nobody wanted to eat fish ever again.

"We need to stop there," Eurylochus said, sauntering over to Odysseus. He stood tall and then so did Odysseus, like they were trying to out-posture each other.

"Out of the question," Odysseus said and turned as if to go back to the helm.

The guys started shouting. Odysseus ignored them. But Eurylochus saw it as the perfect opportunity to take charge. He lowered his head and said something to the guys that I couldn't hear. And then he headed to the back of the boat to where Odysseus stood.

I followed behind him, sticking to the periphery like I did so much of the time.

"There's gonna be mutiny if you don't stop," Eurylochus said.

"Mutiny because of you," Odysseus snapped back. "You

should be siding with me on this. Setting a unified front."

"Why?" Eurylochus said. "I think you're making a horrible decision. We have to stop on this island. Would you just look at it?"

"I don't need to look at it," Odysseus said. "I already know all that I need to know about the island."

"Which is what?"

"Which is that this is the island of Thrinacia. You know, the place where Helios, the sun god, keeps his sacred cattle."

That explained why the sun shone right on the island.

"So what?" Eurylochus said, and he licked his lips at the word 'cattle.'

"*So what* is that we can't eat the cattle," Odysseus said slowly, like he was talking to a three-year-old.

"Fine," Eurylochus said. "We don't eat the cattle. Big deal. We stop. Get some rest. Find some water. Some other food. And then we finish our journey."

"No," Odysseus said.

"Yes," Eurylochus said.

"What part of *no* are you not hearing?" Odysseus said.

"The part that is making you irrational," Eurylochus said. "There is no reason for us to not stop on the island."

"We've been warned to not stop here," Odysseus said. "Not once, but twice."

"Twice," Eurylochus said. "By who? The witch?"

"Circe," Odysseus said, emphasizing her name, "was one of them."

"I'm done listening to the witch," Eurylochus said. "And so are the men."

"Then will they listen to the prophet in the Underworld?" Odysseus said.

"Prophecies are for fools," Eurylochus said.

"You speak lunacy," Odysseus said. "Tiresias himself warned me not to eat the cattle. And Circe herself said there would be only sorrow that would come from us stopping."

"What sorrow?" Eurylochus said. "The men are at their end. They need this. Just look at them, man."

So Odysseus did. And so did I. And I saw what Eurylochus was talking about. The guys had been through horrible things. Terrible things. And I wasn't sure what worse could come. We'd already lost so much. Eurylochus could be right. Just a short little stop on the island.

"Nobody can touch the cattle," Odysseus said, finally relenting. "If they do, I kill them myself."

"As you say," Eurylochus said, and then he left, heading back to the guys to share the good news.

"You think it's the right decision?" I asked Odysseus.

Odysseus kept his eyes on the island of Thrinacia. "No, Bard. I don't."

Peaches and Cream

A HUGE DOCK EXTENDED NEARLY HALF A MILE OUT to sea. The guys steered us close and then tied us to the dock. And when their feet hit the wooden planks, at least seven of them fell to the boards and kissed them.

I didn't kiss the dock, and neither did Dory. Instead, we waited until everyone else had filed off the boat, and then we trailed behind. But when the guys got to the shore and saw, up close, the lush trees filled with fruit, a huge cheer erupted. They started singing a song about how awesome and fantastic Odysseus was. He, of course, raised his hand and waved and smiled and basked in all their attention. But then he glanced around and motioned for them to be quiet.

"The real one you should be thanking is Helios, god of the sun," Odysseus said.

"That's a first," Dory whispered.

I stifled my laugh, but she was right. Odysseus didn't share the spotlight with anyone. Or at least the old Odysseus hadn't. But the last few years had changed all of us.

"He's learning," Polites said, ruffling both of our hair.

Dory shook him off and glared at him.

"Praise Helios, god of the sun!" one of the guys yelled, and they all joined in. And then they all ran for the fruit trees.

I wasn't stupid. The fruit was ripe and plump and looked like it would burst with flavor. And even though there was so much of it—I could have eaten nothing but peaches for the rest of my life on this island—I still was overwhelmed with the feeling that I had to get to it before the guys ate it all. So, I ran through the sand and gorged myself until I couldn't eat another bite. And even after that, I crammed another bite into my mouth and then leaned against the tree and fell asleep.

Ψ

THE GUYS HAD A FIRE GOING WHEN I WOKE UP. I looked around for Dory but couldn't find her anywhere. My heart raced. Now, of all times, they couldn't find out she was a girl. They'd blame her for everything. I wiped the sleep from my eyes and wandered to the fire.

There she was, sitting around the fire, like one of the guys. We really should cut her hair. Or put a do-rag on her or something. Not that guys didn't wear their hair long. It's just that they looked like dudes with longish hair. She looked more and more like a girl.

"Let me repeat," Odysseus was saying. "We do not eat the cattle."

Pork scratched his head. "And why is that again?" Even in the firelight, I could see trails of fruit juice running down his beard and neck.

Odysseus gritted his teeth. "Because they're the sacred cattle of Helios."

"He's a god, right?" Skinner said.

"Yes. He's a god."

"So, we can't eat the cattle," Tailor said. "Can we milk the cattle?"

Milk would have been delicious.

"Do you think golden cattle make golden milk?" I whispered to Dory.

"I don't think so, Homer," she said.

"If they did, do you think it would taste like milk or like gold?" I said.

"It's irrelevant," Dory said. "They don't make golden milk."

"You don't know that," I said.

"We're not going to find out."

"No," Odysseus said. "You cannot milk the cattle."

"Do you think they have golden milk?" Skinner asked.

I smacked Dory on the side. "See, I'm not the only one who thought about it."

"You're comparing yourself to Skinner?" she whispered.

Good point.

"Next question," Odysseus said.

"This is the tenth time he's had to explain it to them," Polites said, sitting down near us.

"So, if we can't eat the cattle or milk the cattle, can we pet the cattle?" Pork asked.

"No. You can't pet the cattle. You can't touch the cattle. Let's just go with this," Odysseus said. "You can't even let your eyes look upon the cattle. Does everyone understand that?"

The guys seemed to consider this.

Finally, Skinner said, "Polites only has one eye. Is he allowed to look at the cattle?"

Odysseus didn't bother responding.

"Here's the plan, men," he said. "We sleep through the night. In the morning, we gather supplies. Cook will let us know how much we need for our short journey back to Ithaca."

I groaned at that.

"We collect the supplies. And then we set off, on our way. Understood?"

The guys nodded. Or at least most of them did, except for Pork.

"If I close my eyes, and happen to stumble into a cow, does that count as touching it?"

Odysseus fixed his eyes on Pork. "Don't. Touch. The. Cattle."

Of all the things I'd be doing in the next twenty-four hours, touching the cattle was not one of them.

"You two should stay near me tonight," Polites said, eyeing the guys. A few of them still cast Dory strange glances, like they knew something was up with her. Or him, since they still thought she was a dude. Or at least I hoped they did.

"You think they know?" I asked as quietly as possible.

"They don't know," Dory said.

But Polites said, "They might. Eurylochus has been stirring up any trouble he can."

That was not a good sign. I wasn't letting Dory out of my sight ever again. If they found out, she'd never even make it to Ithaca. And that was not how I wanted her story to end.

Dory and I each found a soft spot of sand. I'm not sure if Polites ever fell asleep, because I was up long into the night since I'd taken such a huge nap. With his one good eye, he watched the sea. He watched the guys. He watched Odysseus. But he especially watched Eurylochus. And Eurylochus, in turn, watched Dory.

Ψ

WHEN I WOKE UP, IT SOUNDED LIKE THE GODS WERE banging together pots and pans and causing all kinds of mayhem. The sky lit up with lightning, and thunder boomed across the world, rousing me from what had actually been an amazing sleep.

"What now?" I asked. This was getting ridiculous.

"A storm," Polites said, and he stood up and adjusted his sword and belt, like somehow he was off to fight the sky to make it stop.

I nudged Dory with my elbow. How she managed to sleep

through something like this was unreal. Each bang of thunder shook my bones, and the lightning was so bright, even in the dull morning sky, that it left little flashes every time I blinked.

"Why'd you wake me?" Dory said.

I didn't have to answer. The thunder did. And then, the rain started. It poured down from above like pebbles, hitting my head so hard, I thought it might drive right through my skull and into my brain. That would not be good.

We ran for the cover of the fruit trees. And yes, I know that hiding under a tree during a lightning storm isn't such a great idea, but it's not like there was much choice. It was that or get our hair torn off from the rain.

Dory and I sat huddled under one tree. The guys huddled under some others. Eurylochus moved from tree to tree, talking to the guys. And the whole time, Odysseus watched him.

Didn't he see what Eurylochus was up to? He was totally trying to turn everyone on board against Odysseus. And the thing was, even though Eurylochus was an annoying idiot, with every day that went by, a lot of the guys actually listened to him more than they did Odysseus. That wasn't ideal. If they sided with Eurylochus, there was nothing to stop them from taking over the crown once we got back to Ithaca.

"Nothing except the fact that Odysseus is kind of epic," Dory said.

"Epic. Whatever." I kept writing. Almost like magic, the rain stayed off the scroll.

"No really, he is," she said. "None of this would be happening if not for him."

"Exactly," I said. "If he hadn't mouthed off to the cyclops, we'd be home by now. My farm would be saved. And you'd ..." My words trailed off.

"I'd what?" Dory said. "I'd be a slave again? Great. I can hardly wait."

I shook my head. "No. I'm not going to let that happen."

She let out a small laugh that I could barely hear over the thunder. "Right. And what are you doing to do about it?"

I kept writing and didn't meet her eye. "I don't know," I admitted. "But I promise—"

She put up a hand. "Don't make promises you can't keep, Homer."

So, I didn't say anything else. But I didn't give up on it either. There had to be a way to keep Dory from returning to a life of slavery. A way to make everything right.

From under the tree, we watched the water. Waves the size of Titans lapped over the dock and onto the shore. They hit against the ship, and it rocked dangerously close to tipping. All day and all night it rained. And the next morning, when we woke up, the ground was littered with ruined fruit.

WALKING ON SUNSHINE

WE STARED IN HORROR AT THE GROUND. MY STOM-
ach growled, but when I reached out for one of the peaches that
had fallen, it mushed in my hands, like I was trying to grab a
handful of slushie.

The rain on the island had stopped, but almost like the island had a barrier around it, it still raged out on the water. If
anything, the waves were even bigger, reaching as high as the
floating island had been. As long as it kept going, we weren't
going anywhere.

"You realize this is a problem, right?" Dory said.

I slowly nodded, searching the trees with my eyes, looking
for any fruit that wasn't ruined. But if there was even a single
piece, I couldn't find it.

"Maybe we can fish again?" I said.

"Homer, have you seen the water? We can't fish in that."

"I mean once the storm stops," I said. "Then we get on the boat and catch some fish."

When I said we, I meant this in the most general of terms. I was horrible at fishing. No matter where I stood on the ship, it didn't matter. The fish hated me. Dory, on the other hand, they loved her, even though she was the one who actually gutted and cooked them. It was like they were kamikaze fish.

"The storm's not stopping," Eurylochus said, sauntering up like he was already king.

"Of course, it's going to stop," Dory said, getting a little too much up in his face.

He sniffed the air and his eyes narrowed.

"Why do you say that?" he asked her. "Is it some kind of intuition?"

Dory looked at him like he'd been hit on the head with one too many raindrops. "No. It's common sense. Rain doesn't keep going on forever."

"Hmmm …," he said.

"This is Zeus' doing," Odysseus said, walking up. He stood tall, but his face looked like he was nearing his breaking point.

"It's not Zeus' doing," Eurylochus said. "It's your doing. You're the one who brought all this on us in the first place."

"No," Odysseus said. "It is not my fault at all."

Side note, Odysseus really did need to start owning up, just a bit. Because the gods had no reason to be mad at anyone else. But I kept my mouth shut.

"Then maybe it's someone else's fault," Eurylochus said, and he turned to look directly at Dory.

"What?" she said, putting her hands on her hips, and I cringed. Of all the things she shouldn't do right now.

Almost like she heard my thoughts, she quickly dropped her hands to her sides.

Eurylochus scowled at her.

I quickly stepped in front of her, like somehow, all four foot eight of me was going to protect her.

"You know, it's not really helping anything to sit here arguing about it," I said.

All eyes turned to me.

"The bard is right," Odysseus said. "What we need to do is take action."

"Action like what?" Eurylochus said. "Maybe there's another cyclops we can blind."

Anger flared on Odysseus' face, but amazingly he kept his temper. "Perhaps next time I'll make a deal with the cyclops and feed him you to appease him."

I wasn't going to say it, but it would have made our entire journey a lot easier. Without Eurylochus around, we might've been home by now.

Might've. It wasn't the word I wanted to be using. But all I knew is that we had to get off this island, or we'd never get home.

"What action do you suggest then?" Eurylochus said.

Odysseus crossed his arms over his barrel chest. "I'll pray to Zeus. Ask him to stop this storm." And without another word, he walked away, leaving me and Dory with Eurylochus. The guy made my skin crawl. And I knew he suspected what was up with Dory.

"Come on," I said, grabbing Dory's arm. "There must be some fruit left we can pick up."

I didn't want to go scavenging for mush fruit, but I did want to get away from Eurylochus.

"Don't wander too far," Eurylochus said. "It's dangerous out there."

"It's the island of Helios," I said. "The sun god. He keeps cattle here. It's not dangerous."

A small smile formed on Eurylochus' face. "Danger can come from anywhere."

Or anyone, I thought.

I dragged Dory back to the trees. "Are you insane? Are you trying to get killed?"

"I hate that guy," she said.

I shook my head. "That's not the point. You can't let your guard down now. Not when we're this close to getting home."

Dory bit her lip and looked to the ground.

"What?" I said.

She shook her head. "Nothing."

"Tell me," I said.

"I said it's nothing." But then she swiped at her face. It left a streak that had nothing to do with the offshore storm.

Oh crap. Dory was crying. I was completely not equipped to handle this. Sure, Mom cried from time to time, but she always thought I wasn't watching, and I always pretended I wasn't. I think she missed Dad. A lot. But here, now, with Dory ... I couldn't pretend I didn't see.

My empty stomach knotted. "What's wrong, Dory?"

She wiped another tear but didn't say anything.

"Tell me," I said.

Dory took a huge breath. "Homer, I don't want to go home."

I let out something like a nervous laugh that sounded more like a wimpy little cough.

"I'm serious, Homer. I don't want to get back."

"I know," I said. "We've talked about that."

But she shook her head. "There's more."

"What more?"

"I've been working against us," she said. "Doing little things to delay our journey."

"You have not," I said. "That whole girl-on-a-ship-brings-bad-luck thing is a total wives' tale."

"Not that," Dory said. "I'm the one who cut the holes in the sail."

"That was the wind," I said.

Dory shook her head. "It wasn't the wind."

My eyes widened. "It was you?"

She nodded. "And I threw food overboard, making us have to stop at Circe's island."

"You did not!"

"I did," Dory said. "And ... I let the wind out of the bag."

"No. Way." I couldn't believe it. Dory seemed so ... innocent.

"It's why we've had such a horrible journey," Dory said. "I don't want to get home. I'm not going back to be a slave again."

"I'm not going to let you be a slave again. Remember."

"Don't you get it, Homer? I've always been a slave. I always will be. There's nothing you can do about it. Not one thing."

"There is," I said.

"What?"

I poured through my brain, really trying to come up with something. But no matter what I thought of, it came down to the fact that Mom and I were only one scroll away from being slaves ourselves.

"I don't know," I said. "Maybe we can ask Odysseus to help. He's a king. Maybe he can do something."

Dory shook her head. Her tears had stopped, though her face still looked really red and streaky. "Once we get to Ithaca, I'm staying. You can go back to Ionia without me."

"No," I said.

"Yes," Dory said. "It's the only solution."

It was completely not the only solution. But despite my best efforts, I couldn't think of anything better. But still … the thought of leaving Dory behind, of never seeing her again … It left a horrible pit in my stomach that I was pretty sure would never go away.

$$\Psi$$

ODYSSEUS WENT OFF TO THE HILLS TO PRAY. OR maybe he was just sitting around doing nothing, because the storm continued on for hours. Days. The guys tried fishing, but with the waves crashing around nearly drowning them with every hit, they gave up pretty soon. So, they gobbled up what mush fruit they could, but the flies got to it also. And then they started catching flies. And that's when the grumbling that was boiling just below the surface really took off.

"You know why there are flies on this island?" Skinner said.

"Because it's stinky," Pork answered.

It was stinky, that was for sure. No one was going near the water to wash off, and since we couldn't go near the cattle, we didn't venture far from the beach.

"It's because of the cows," Skinner said. "And if there are cows on this island, then why are we trying to eat flies?"

"Because Odysseus told us not to eat the cows," Pork said.

"But think of the brisket. The steak. The bacon," Skinner said.

"Cows don't make bacon," Pork said.

Even though we'd all nearly been turned into pigs, my stomach still rumbled at the word "bacon." What I wouldn't give to be back in Ionia right now with Mom making me a plate of bacon and eggs.

"They must have some kind of bacon," Skinner said. "We should eat them to find out."

"We can't eat the cows," Pork said.

"Have you seen them?" Eurylochus said, walking up right then. By now most of the guys were listening. Dory and I sat off to the side, me writing and her digging in the dirt for roots we could eat.

"Seen who?" Skinner said.

"The cattle," Eurylochus said.

Pork shook his head. "We can't look at the cows. Remember?"

After his unending questions on the matter, I was surprised that he remembered.

Eurylochus smiled his weasel smile. "There is no harm that can come from gazing upon the cattle. The only reason Odysseus told us not to was so he could keep them all for himself."

"He did?" Skinner said.

"No way," Pork said.

"That's not true," Dory said, speaking up, even though I wished she would keep her mouth shut. "You aren't supposed to go near them or else Helios will get angry."

"They are gold like the sun," Eurylochus said, ignoring

Dory's words. "They shine with an internal brightness, and they are three time the size of a normal cow. Juicy and plump. And there are so many of them."

The guys' mouths hung open, and half of them were drooling. Fine, I was drooling, too.

"It couldn't hurt to just look at them," Skinner said.

"Just look," Pork said.

And that's all it took. Dory tried to tell everyone to stop, but there was no reasoning with forty hungry stomachs. So Eurylochus led them through the trees. Dory and I trailed behind with Polites.

"This is not a good idea, Homer," she said. "This is so not a good idea."

"They're just going to look at the cattle," I said.

"They're not," Polites said. "When they see the cattle, they won't be able to resist."

"It would be a nice time for Odysseus to get back," I said. He'd been gone for days now. What did he expect? Of course, the guys were going to get hungry. Even I wanted to eat the cattle.

"Can you go find him?" Dory asked Polites.

But I wasn't sure that was such a great idea. "You should stay here," I said. "Make sure the guys don't touch the cows. I'll go find Odysseus."

We went back and forth on it a few times, and then it was too late because from up ahead of us, the guys let out a huge roar. We ran as fast as we could to catch up, but it wasn't fast enough.

They'd pushed through the wooden fence holding in the cattle, and they ran forward, knives drawn. Before the sound of Polites' shouts could even reach them, five of the cows were down. And then it was too late.

Dory sank to the ground, against a tree. "This is horrible. Awful. Terrible. We are so doomed."

But there was no doing anything about it now. The men dragged the cows back to the beach and made a fire, and I guess it was the smell of the burning meat that drew Odysseus back because he came running from the hills, waving his arms.

"Stop!" he shouted, but the damage was done.

The sun blasted and blared through the sky, heating up with each second that passed. The clouds swirled around it, creating a tunnel of light directed right at the guys on the beach.

"What part of *'don't eat the cattle'* did you not understand?" Odysseus said. He paced back and forth on the beach. And at his words, and the realization that the guys were now being burned alive by the sun, the meat dropped from their hands.

"I tried to stop them," Eurylochus said.

"You liar!" Dory screamed. "You egged them on. This is all your fault."

"This is all your fault," Eurylochus sneered back at Dory, and I knew in that instant that he knew about Dory being a girl. He'd throw her overboard as soon as we were back in the ship.

"We need to leave," Odysseus said.

"But the storm," Polites said.

"Can't be helped," Odysseus said. And so we dragged

ourselves down the dock, grasping onto the wood to keep from being swept over, until we got to the ship.

The sun stalked us to the edge of the dock, but once we got aboard, it slipped back behind the clouds, as if to mock us into thinking we were safe. And then, in further mockery, no sooner had we pulled away from the dock, the raging storm ended, bringing a quiet calm that unsettled me. A calm that forebode horror to come.

We all wanted to believe in the calm, so once we were far enough away from the island that we could hardly see the sun shining overhead, we breathed again.

That's when Eurylochus cornered Dory.

SPIN ME RIGHT ROUND

DORY WAS IN THE GALLEY, COMING UP WITH ANY-thing that might help us eat. I sat in my normal place, on the bench in the corner, writing down everything that had gone on.

"Make sure you get all the dialogue right," Dory said. "Dialogue is really important."

"I'm getting it as right as I can," I said. "But I have to translate it into Dactylic Hexameter. That's not as easy as it sounds."

Okay, this was kind of a lie. Dactylic Hexameter was getting easier with every line I wrote. I'd gotten to the point where I used it in everyday conversation, because it was fun.

Eurylochus poked his slimy head into the galley. "Odysseus needs you up on deck," he said.

I stood up. Odysseus probably wanted to make sure I was shining the best light on him after the cattle incident. And I'll admit. This time, with the cows ... it was totally not his fault.

"Not you, Bard," Eurylochus said. "He wants the cook."

Dory looked up from the floury mess in front of her. I guess she was making hardtack or something equally unsavory.

"Why?" I asked, even as she dusted off her hands on her ripped and faded pants. Something about the request didn't settle right. Why would Odysseus send Eurylochus, of all people, to get Dory? As far as I could tell Odysseus and Eurylochus were minutes away from an epic duel that only one of them would sail away from.

"None of your business, Bard," Eurylochus said.

"Actually, everything that happens on this ship is my business," I said. "It's why I'm here."

"Not this," Eurylochus said. "Just the cook."

So, Dory followed him out of the galley, but there was no way I was going to just sit there. I crept after them, up the narrow ladder that led to the side of the ship. When I peeked my head around the corner to where they stood, my heart stopped in my chest.

"You are the entire reason we aren't home yet," Eurylochus said.

Dory rolled her eyes. "That's ridiculous."

"It's not," Eurylochus said. "You've brought bad luck to us. You. It's all been you."

He knew.

Dory knew he knew because her eyes widened.

I stumbled forward, trying to reach them before he did

something, but my shirt caught on a splinter. I yanked at it, to get it free, but as I did, Eurylochus grabbed Dory by the arm and started dragging her toward the railing.

"Stop!" I screamed, and I yanked at my shirt, ripping a huge part of it off.

"I'll throw you over, too," Eurylochus said. "You knew she was a girl. You've brought the bad luck to us, too."

There was no way he was throwing either of us over. I lunged for Dory and managed to grab her leg, dropping her to the ground. Eurylochus lost his grip but reached out again. I rolled us both out of the way.

He stepped forward. And he pulled his sword out. This was it. We were both dead. I tensed every muscle in my body and waited for the feeling of steel ripping through me.

Then, into his path stepped Polites.

Waves of relief flooded through me.

"You don't go near them," Polites said, and he pulled his own sword.

But adrenaline pumped through Eurylochus, fueling him. Before Polites could even react, Eurylochus lifted his sword and ran it through Polites' middle.

Dory screamed. I heard myself scream, too. And then Eurylochus pulled his sword from Polites' body. He fell backwards to the deck.

"You killed him!" Dory screamed.

"And you'll be next," Eurylochus said.

Polites was dead.

There was no one and nothing to stop him now. He was going to kill us both.

But Odysseus must've heard our screams, because he rounded the corner, sword already in his hand. He stumbled to a halt as his eyes found Polites, motionless on the deck. Blood still dripped from Eurylochus' sword.

"What have you done, man?" Odysseus bellowed.

"He got in my way," Eurylochus said.

"You killed him," Odysseus said.

"He knew why our luck never turned," Eurylochus said. "He knew what not even you know, oh great and knowledgeable king of kings." His voice dripped with sarcasm.

"What? That the cook is girl?" Odysseus said. "Of course, I knew that."

Eurylochus' eyes widened. "And you let her stay on board? You brought us the bad luck yourself. It's your fault as much as it is hers." He advanced forward.

Dory and I stayed motionless. There was no good that would come from us getting in the middle of this fight. It had been coming forever.

"It is the fault of the gods," Odysseus said, and he stepped forward, matching Eurylochus, ready to carry through with what he should have done so long ago.

"Curse the gods!" Eurylochus screamed, and then he lunged forward.

Except then a huge bolt of lightning streaked down, hitting the main sail. The gods had heard Eurylochus, and they were not happy.

The mast cracked in half and fell right for Eurylochus, even as Odysseus swiped out with his sword. But Eurylochus jumped out of the way, evading his double fate.

The lightning struck again. And again. This was not only because of Eurylochus. This was Zeus' revenge for Helios. The price we had to pay for eating the cows. The punishment we'd hoped and prayed would never be delivered. It had finally come.

"Row, men!" Odysseus bellowed, even as Eurylochus came at him again, oblivious to the destruction around him.

A rope broke, and another sail swung around, hitting Eurylochus square in the chest, sending him flying backward into the wood.

The boat careened off course, no matter how hard the guys tried to row. The sail was ruined. Our speed increased, pulled by the waves and the wind. The guys fought against it, but the gods were too strong. Too angry.

In front of us, the two monsters materialized, as if we'd been sucked right toward them. The curse from Poseidon. Scylla on the right and Charybdis on the left. The trouble we thought we'd already left behind.

The wind whipped and drove us right for the swirling, gaping mouth of Charybdis.

"I'm sorry for failing you, men," Odysseus said because there was nothing that could get us out of this. It was the perfect storm. The point of no return. We swirled around three times, as if Charybdis was teasing us. And then our ship was swallowed by the monster.

GREEK LETTERS

WATER GUSHED AROUND ME. I WAS SUCKED UNDER. I tried not to breathe in the briny water, but it splashed down my throat because it was everywhere. My eyes stung. My lungs burned. I struggled to reach the surface.

"Dory!" I shouted once I got there. I could hardly see from all the mist in the air.

No response.

"Dory!" I shouted again, but I couldn't even hear the sound of my own voice. The monster's roars filled my ears. I was pulled under again.

Below the surface, the world was a mass of frothing bubbles. I tore against them with my arms, again trying to reach the surface, but the monster pulled me down, exactly the opposite of the way I wanted to go. The way I needed to go if I wanted to stay alive. And then the bubbles cleared and I wish they hadn't because I saw some of the guys farther down, getting sucked one by one into the gaping mouth of the beast. Pork. Skinner. Tailor.

Charybdis was finally getting her chance.

I had to find Dory. Odysseus. I had to find a way out of this.

A dark shape flew by me, getting sucked down faster than anything else around. I only had a second to see the wide eyes of Eurylochus before Charybdis swallowed him whole.

I didn't feel even the slightest regret.

I pulled at the water again with my arms and finally broke the surface. The fog had cleared, but so had everything else. There was no sign of the ship. No sign of anyone or anything. I was completely alone.

The water got really quiet and still, and I took what might have been the only chance I had. I swam away from the monster. But I couldn't head toward Scylla either. I'd seen what she could do. My foot kicked at something hard which then slammed into my knee while it was surfacing. I grabbed hold without looking. Maybe it was another shark, and this time it was going to eat me. I didn't care. I didn't have any energy left to worry about it. If I hadn't been so tired, I might have been relieved to see that it was only a piece of wood. But then I saw what was on it. A golden Greek letter. Omega. The end. Part of the wall from our storage area on the ship. I clutched hard to it, wrapping my arms and legs around it, and I let it carry me away.

A Heroic Divergence

I WOKE UP ON A BEACH AND STUMBLED TO MY FEET. I scanned the area for anyone. Anything. It only took me a second to find Dory, curled up on the beach, with her arms and legs still wrapped around a tree.

I ran over to her as fast as I could in the thick sand.

"Dory!" I said, shaking her.

Nothing.

Oh gods, please don't let her be dead. That was not how this story was supposed to end. I was not going to write that.

"Dory!" I said again, and I shook her harder.

This time she stirred a little and said something I couldn't understand.

"What?" I said. "I can't hear you."

She mumbled again.

"Dory? Are you okay? Speak to me!"

She finally rolled over enough that her mouth wasn't pressed into the sand.

"I said to stop shaking me," she said. "I'm aching all over."

I laughed and then grabbed her in a hug before I even gave it a second of thought.

"I am so glad you aren't dead," I said, and that's when the memories came rushing back.

Polites, dead at the hand of Eurylochus. Odysseus, confronting the murderer. The curse from the gods. The guys being pulled downward. The gaping mouth of Charybdis. The splintered ship.

"Did you see?" I asked.

Dory nodded but didn't say a word.

"I don't like this story anymore," I said.

"I don't either, Homer, but sometimes people have to write things that make them cry."

"I'm not crying," I said, forcing away the tears that were ready to burst.

"I know," Dory said.

I felt in my pocket for the scroll because I wanted to get away from the sad stuff. I could reread parts of the story that made me laugh. Parts about the guys trying to fish. Or some of the jokes they told. Or the incessant farting. But my pocket was empty.

"It's gone," I said, not wanting to voice the words.

But a small smile crept onto Dory's face.

"What?"

"I found it, Homer. In the water. When the ship went down." And she reached into her own pocket and pulled out my scroll.

I've never been so happy to see anything in my entire life. I almost grabbed the scroll and hugged it, too.

"Oh my gods," I said. "You are the best friend in the entire universe!"

"I know," Dory said and handed it over. And amazingly every single word I'd written was still on there, perfectly scripted. Well, I guess as perfect as my messy handwriting allowed it to be. The lines showing how many days we'd been on our journey were still inked in the margins.

"You've saved my life," I said. "You know that, right?" Without the scroll, there was no point in going on. My entire future depended on this scroll.

"Maybe not," Dory said. "Have you looked around?"

I clutched the scroll in my hands, because I was never going to let it go again, and finally studied the world around me. The sand was white like sparkling crystals and went on forever in both directions. In front of us was the water, completely still, almost mocking us for the horrific whirlpool we'd just survived. And behind us were dunes. Whatever was behind the dunes, we couldn't see.

"Any clue where we are?" I asked.

"Well, I'm pretty sure it's not Ionia," Dory said.

I'd been to the beaches near Ionia enough times to know she was right. They had way darker sand, and the beaches were always crowded with families and kids. Back when Dad had been alive, we'd been one of those families, visiting the shore for fun on the weekends. But there was nothing fun about our current situation.

"Maybe Ithaca?" I said.

Dory pulled her eyebrows together. "You saw Ithaca. It had way more rocks than beaches."

I knew she was right.

"Perfect. So it's not Ionia, and it's not Ithaca. Where does that leave us?"

"Completely out of luck?" Dory said.

"Great pep talk. You should start writing inspirational books."

Dory punched me on the shoulder which really hurt because I already felt like I'd been punched in every muscle of my entire body.

"We should go exploring," I said. "See if anyone else survived." I hated to say those words because I knew the truth.

But Dory didn't have the same hesitation. "No one else survived," she said.

The truth sat there in the air between us and taunted us. Everyone else was dead.

Except then something miraculous happened. Someone came walking from up over the dunes.

"King Odysseus!" Dory said, even now remembering to use his royal title, and she ran toward him.

He waved when he saw us, but sadness covered his face.

Sadness that echoed the death of all his guys. Sadness in know-ing that he felt responsible. That he'd lost everything. And with that sadness, my hopes for the future slipped away.

"Where are we?" Dory asked once we reached him.

He lifted his mournful eyes and gazed out at the calm wa-ter. "They're dead. They're all dead. Even Polites, my dearest friend. We've been together forever. Fought side by side. The man lost an eye for me. Gave up his life and his family to come on this journey. To help me in my time of greatest need. And for what? To be killed at the hands of a traitor."

"He died protecting me," Dory said. "He was a really, really great guy, and I'm going to miss him."

Odysseus put his head in his hand. "I've failed him. I've failed them all. I should have died with them. Should have gone down with my ship to pay for my mistakes."

Dory shook her head. "No. The gods kept you alive. They kept us alive."

"We may as well be dead."

"But we're not," Dory said.

"Maybe not," Odysseus said, "But this is the end, my beau-tiful friends. We can't go on. I can't go on."

"Sure you can," I said. I didn't know about Odysseus, but I still had every intention of getting home. Mom needed me. And I was still going to be a soldier. Or was I? With all that had happened, that future felt like a childish dream.

"No, young Bard," Odysseus said. "This is the end of the journey." And he sank to the sand and buried his face in his hands.

Dory looked like she wanted to choke him.

"What is he doing?" she whispered. "He's just giving up?"

If Odysseus heard her, he made no visible sign.

"He's really sad," I said.

"We're all really sad," Dory said. "Sad things happen. That doesn't mean we just kick over and die."

"He feels like a failure," I said.

"That's because he is a failure," Dory said. "But, so what? People fail all the time, at everything. That doesn't mean he should just quit."

I knew she was right, but I also got the failure thing. If I didn't get back to Ionia—if I failed—I wasn't sure what I would do.

"Just give him a few minutes," I said. "Polites was his best friend."

Just like Dory was my best friend. I didn't want to think about her being gone.

Dory scampered to the top of a nearby dune and looked inward, away from the endless water.

"Is that a building over there?" she asked, loud enough that Odysseus had to hear.

"The gods, mocking us once more," Odysseus said, barely looking up from his hands.

"No, really," Dory said. "There's definitely something over there."

And I guess this was enough to pique his interest because

223

he got up, and we trundled in the direction Dory pointed.

I'm not going to go deep into the story here. I'll summarize it as this.

Odysseus of course went into the building which was built into the side of a hill like a cave, and he met some woman named Calypso. I guess she was some kind of sea nymph who happened to be the daughter of Atlas. For those who don't know, he was one of the Titans. So, she was immortal. And I guess she wanted Odysseus to become immortal, too.

Dory and I set up camp inside a small cave conveniently located a bit away from the main dwelling place of Calypso.

But Odysseus was a complete depressed mess. He moped around day after day after day. Months went by. Maybe even a year. I stopped making marks in the margin of the scroll because it seemed stupid at this point. I flipped the hourglass only once, so it couldn't have been that long.

Thankfully Dory agreed to keep on cooking. Otherwise, I would have resorted to seaweed and coconuts, probably not the most well-rounded of diets. And while Dory cooked, I got caught up on the story, writing every detail, revising the parts I'd already written, filling in more info on the characters. I spent a good amount of time on Polites because the guy deserved it. He'd given up his life protecting me and Dory, and even though being stuck on this island was kind of boring, we were at least still alive.

Ψ

"YOU SHOULD GO TALK TO ODYSSEUS," DORY SAID. "Tell him we need to leave. I may not want to go back to Ionia, but we can't stay here any longer."

She'd been nagging me incessantly to go do this, but I wanted to get caught up on the story first. I still had plenty of time. But finally, I couldn't put it off anymore.

So, I tried. A bunch of times. But every time I asked Odysseus about it, he said something vague like, "We can think about that tomorrow, Bard," or, "There's plenty of time to worry about that later, Bard." He also said some things that weren't quite so positive like, "What's the point in ever leaving?" or, "I've ruined everything. I don't deserve to go on." The sun didn't seem to shine quite so bright on these days.

And the whole time Calypso sang songs that seemed to hypnotize Odysseus and wove carpets and blankets on a giant golden loom. Odysseus was beyond hope.

"You're right," I finally said to Dory after a particularly futile day of trying to convince Odysseus to leave. "We're never getting off of this island."

I sank down into a bench and rolled the scroll up tight, shoving it back into my pocket. I'd written all the words there were to write. There wasn't anything more to add.

"Maybe ...," Dory said.

"Maybe what?" I put my head between my hands and

225

moped properly.

"Maybe we can do something … oh, I don't know … proactive."

"Proactive?" I mumbled into my hands.

"Yeah, proactive," Dory said. "That's what heroes in stories do. They take charge of the situation and make things happen. They don't wait for things to happen to them."

I lifted my head and met her eyes. "But we're not the hero of this story. Odysseus is."

She looked at me like a coconut had fallen on my head one too many times. "Yeah, maybe, but you're writing the story, right? What if we could be the heroes of the story, just for a little bit?"

Her words floated around in my mind. "But Odysseus …"

"… isn't doing jack squat," Dory said. "We need to take action for him. Get ourselves out of this situation. We need to get this story back on track."

I had no clue how Dory was always right about this stuff, but there was nothing I could find wrong about what she was saying. I was the storyteller. I could do whatever I wanted with the story. And if the story demanded a temporary hero, then I was going to give it one.

"Okay, so what do we do?"

We sat around and brainstormed for the next couple days, writing down every idea we came up with. Sure, there were some pretty basic ideas, like running into Calypso's house and grabbing Odysseus and dragging him out of there or building giant wings and flying away or tricking Calypso into magically sending us home, but most of these weren't feasible. Still, just the brainstorming process made us come up with a lot of things we might not have thought about otherwise. Finally, at the end of the week of brainstorming, we had a plan.

THE COCONUT OWL

"MAKE AN OFFERING TO ATHENA?" I SAID. "YOU'RE sure that's the best plan?"

Dory had been stuck on this idea forever.

"Nothing you came up with is any better, Homer."

I glanced at the most recent sketch I'd made. "I don't know. This one has serious potential."

"A raft made out of coconut shells?"

"It would float," I said.

"Coconut shells have holes in them," Dory said.

"We could patch those."

"No, Homer. Just no."

"Fine. So, we make an offering to Athena. Maybe she likes coconuts," I said, letting the sarcasm drip off my tongue.

Dory smacked me on the shoulder. It hurt. "That's a great

idea, Homer."

"I was kidding."

"No, it'll be really creative," Dory said. "I have the best idea."

So, we spent the next week crafting the perfect offering. We had plenty of time so that wasn't an issue, and I admit that by the end of the week, I was into the plan, too. Our offering was perfect and awesome, and Athena was going to love it.

"You're sure the eyes aren't too big?" Dory said as I placed the final one.

"Owls have huge eyes," I said and wedged the final eye into place.

And then we both stepped back to admire our work of art. In front of us was the most bodacious owl constructed from coconut shells in the entire world. And then we prayed because we wanted to make sure we got her attention. I did not want to be a failure before I'd even become a teenager.

My prayers went something like, "Please help us get off this boring island, or I am going to go completely insane." Sure, I also added some more serious stuff about how I had to get home to Mom and tell her about Dad and how I really wanted to see her again and how I didn't want her disappointment to be the last thing she remembered about having me as a son. But I kept these prayers to myself.

Not a day later, while we were on the beach praying, Hermes strolled up.

"You can stop praying to her," Hermes said. "She's heard you since the first day."

"Did she like the owl?" Dory asked.

"She loved the owl," Hermes said. "She's been bragging about it to all the other gods."

"It's made completely of coconuts," I said.

"Yeah, we've heard that from her about a hundred times," Hermes said. "Athena loves coconuts. You kids did good."

"Does that mean she's going to help us?" Dory said, but it was weird the way she phrased it. Like maybe praying to get off the island wasn't her only prayer either. But if I had my own private prayers, Dory must also.

"Why do you think I'm here?" Hermes said.

"Because you're going to take us back to Ionia right now?" I said. Hope filled my words. That would be so much better than floating away on a raft.

"No, Homer," Hermes said. "What kind of story ending would that be?"

"A really good one?"

"Not good enough," Hermes said. "Plus, the story isn't over yet. Odysseus isn't home."

"So, you can magically take him back, too," I said.

Hermes shook his head. "Not today. But I am going to politely ask Calypso to let Odysseus go."

"You're going to politely ask her?" I said. "Are you kidding? She'll say no. She's a crazy, psychotic deity who's woven two hundred rugs in the last year."

"Last seven years," Hermes said.

"Ha ha. Not funny."

"What's not funny?" Hermes said.

"Seven years." I held up my hourglass. I still had only flipped it the one time since we'd been on the island.

Hermes leaned forward to get a closer look and tapped on the glass. A huge clump of sand seemed to break free, and the remaining sand in the hourglass whooshed to the bottom.

I almost choked on a piece of seaweed.

"It was stuck," he said.

Stuck. Was he kidding? That was not good.

"How much time has really passed?" Dory asked.

"Seven years, like I said," Hermes said. "Which means you have about a week to get home."

"A week! But …"

"But what?"

"But that's not enough time," I said. "That can't be right."

"And yet it is," Hermes said, twirling his hat. The wings spread out wide and then settled back down.

It was the worst news possible. One week. How could seven years have gone by on this stupid island? Seven years!

Hermes grinned. "But I do have a direct order from Zeus here telling Calypso she has to let Odysseus go. She'll have to say yes, whether she wants to or not."

"And then we'll go home?" I said.

"That's the plan," Hermes said. "If Odysseus can evade Poseidon and make it to Ithaca, the story will be over."

Now that was good news. Finally. Of course, the *"if Odysseus can evade Poseidon"* part wasn't going to be the easiest task in the world, but maybe since we had Athena's blessing, Poseidon would leave us alone.

Hermes headed for Calypso's house, so I took the opportunity to update the story. Finally, after weeks of nothing, I had something new to add.

I'd just finished getting the first draft of the new part down when Hermes came out of the house with Odysseus, looking fresh and groomed and all put together, and Calypso trailing behind him.

Let's put it this way. Calypso did not look happy. Not at all. Instead she looked like she'd swallowed a giant bullfrog and it had lodged in her throat. Her dark face was red, and she looked so angry, I thought she would have yanked Hermes' winged hat off and hit him upside the head with it.

But Odysseus? His face glowed like it hadn't since we set out from Troy ten years ago.

"You can't do this," Calypso said, and she stomped her foot like she was ready to have a giant tantrum.

"I can and I did," Hermes said. "It's time for Odysseus to go."

"But he's supposed to stay here forever and ever and ever," Calypso said. "That means always." She balled up her fists, like she was channeling the anger through them. But then, her face shifted, and large tears formed in the corners of her eyes. And she started bawling. Ugly crying. Huge sobs escaped from her mouth, and she fell to her knees in the sand and begged and pleaded with Odysseus for him to stay.

But Odysseus was a changed man. He patted her head like

a child and told her that he would miss her but that he had to leave. That he had responsibilities back on Ithaca that could not be forgotten, no matter how much he might want to spend the rest of his life here on her island (Ogygia was its name, by the way).

But in the end, Calypso had no choice but to agree. So, she gave us some food and water and showed us a bunch of logs and rope that was even more perfect for making a raft than coconuts, and then she ran back to her house crying the entire time, like she thought somehow that would make Odysseus change his mind.

There was no changing it. Once the raft was finished, a huge grin formed on his face.

"Bard. Cook. Let's show Poseidon who's boss."

I hated the way he phrased that. Even now, he was still mocking Poseidon? And I got this horrible, awful feeling that I shouldn't climb on the raft. That I should run back to the house I'd been living in for the last seven years and just stay there. Except that's when I looked at the hourglass hanging around my neck. There wasn't much sand left. One week. We had to leave.

So Dory, Odysseus, and I climbed onto the raft and cast away from the island of Calypso. But no sooner was the island out of sight, a giant wave came. A last gift from Poseidon. The raft turned upside-down and smacked me hard on the head. Everything went black.

Blinded by the Light

OKAY, LET'S GO BACK TO THAT OTHER CHAPTER where I woke up on the beach. Yeah, this one is really pretty similar except when I woke up, I was face up in the sand. The sun warmed me from above, and I could see its brightness from behind my closed eyes. Also, I was alive. I don't want to minimize this part, because it made me happy. Unless I was really dead this time and in the Underworld. But I'd been to the Underworld, or at least part of it. This didn't smell like death and rot. It smelled like the beach. Also, my head throbbed with so much pain, I had to be alive. I ran my fingers over the spot. There was a goose egg the size of … well, a goose egg for lack of a better description. I could almost hear Dory telling me to not be lazy in my similes, but it hurt too much to think of anything else.

I opened my eyes so I could get a better view of my surroundings because, alive or not, if we were back on Calypso's island, I was going to scream. Seriously scream. Except when I tried to open my eyes, I realized that they were already opened. I just couldn't see anything except the pure white of the sun.

I turned my head left and right. I tried holding my eyelids open with my fingers. But it didn't make a difference. I was completely blind.

LOST BUT NOT FORGOTTEN

"DORY?" I SAID.

"I'm right here, Homer."

I turned my head in the direction of her voice, but I didn't see anything.

"Where?"

"Right here. Like five feet away from you."

Five feet away? All I saw was white.

"I can't see you." I tried to keep the quivering out of my voice, but it was useless. This was horrible, awful.

"What do you mean, you can't see me?" she asked.

I swallowed a huge lump in my throat. "I mean that I can't see you. I can't see anything."

I heard some shuffling and then felt Dory's hand on my arm.

"Here I am, Homer. Right here."

I grabbed her hand with my other hand without thinking. And I didn't let go. Because I had to know she was there.

"I think I'm blind," I said. Blind and completely and utterly hosed.

"It's just the sun, Homer. It's probably a temporary thing."

I wanted to believe her. I really did. But everything felt pretty hopeless right now. I'd been hit on the head by the raft, and it had made me go blind.

"What do you see?" I asked. "Odysseus?"

She didn't say anything at first, and then she said, "Oh, sorry."

"For what?"

"I nodded but you didn't see me. Yeah, I see Odysseus. We're on a beach. He's sitting there looking like the world has come to an end."

"And has it?"

"No, Homer," Dory said. "The world has not come to an end. We're on a beach, but there are all sorts of buildings, and I can even see people from here."

"So, we're somewhere?"

She laughed. "Yeah, we're somewhere."

"Do they look like they're going to eat us?" I asked.

"No."

"Attack us?"

"Nope."

"Tear us limb from limb?"

"Not at all, Homer."

That, at least, was good news.

I patted the front of my shirt, like I'd done for the entire journey, but the scroll wasn't there.

"Do you have it again?" I asked.

"Have what?"

"The scroll. It's gone." This was no different than last time. Dory had probably grabbed it when we landed on this beach.

There was a pause again that I hoped was Dory nodding her head, but then she said, "No, Homer. I don't have it."

"Ha ha. You're kidding."

"I'm not kidding. I don't have it."

That's when the real panic set in. I patted at my shirt again and felt the sand all around me, but I couldn't see anything. And if I thought I was hosed before because I couldn't see, then I was fifty gazillion times that hosed right now. If I couldn't find the scroll, everything was lost.

"You have to help me find it," I said. "Please."

Dory patted my arm. "Don't worry, Homer. You sit right here. I'll search the beach for it."

And so she set off, and I sat there and tried completely unsuccessfully not to panic. I could not lose the scroll.

"Did you find it?" I asked, hoping she was in earshot.

"Not yet."

I waited a few more minutes.

"Did you find it now?"

"Not yet."

I listened to the gulls flying overhead, trying to focus on all the little noises around me, but all I could think about was the stupid scroll.

"Okay, how about now?"

"Listen, Homer. I'll tell you when I find it. Just stay here. I'm heading farther down the beach near where Odysseus is."

"You'll come back?" I asked.

She leaned down and gave me a quick hug. Almost like it wasn't even a hug. Except that it was. And then it was over.

"I'll come back."

And so, I sat and waited. I traced my hands through the sand, making designs I couldn't see. I listened to the waves hitting up against the beach. They came from my left which meant that if I wanted to make it to people, I should head right, just in case Dory didn't come back. Except she would come back. She would not leave me here.

After the longest ten minutes in the history of the universe, I finally heard her voice again.

She must've sat down in the sand in front of me because she grabbed both my hands.

"Homer, I can't find it."

Her words entered my mind and twisted around like fog filling in all the spaces. They were horrible words. Words I didn't want to be true. I wanted to take those words back and throw them away.

"Please please please tell me you're kidding," I said.

"I wish I was," she said. "But I looked everywhere. There is no sign of anything that even looks like bits and pieces of it. The scroll is gone."

No. I was not going to give up yet.

"Did you ask Odysseus?"

Small silence. Maybe she was nodding her head again?

"He left the beach before I could," Dory said. "He headed into town."

A small flicker of hope filled me. "So he could have it."

"I don't know, Homer. He wasn't carrying anything. And his yellow tunic was in complete tatters, just like ours."

I didn't care if my clothes fell off me at this point. This was it. The end of the journey. There was no point to go on from here.

"How is the hourglass?" I asked. "Is there any sand left?"

Another small silence. Then, "It's almost empty," Dory said. "We can't have more than a couple days left."

A couple days. A week. A month. It didn't matter. With no scroll, there was no story. And with no story, my future was dead.

"I'm never going to get back to Ionia, Dory," I said, as the horrible truth set in. Everything I'd wanted was pointless. I couldn't do anything to save Mom. I was a complete and utter failure.

"You know what, Homer?"

"What?"

"Let's not worry about it right now. Let's go into town and find something to eat."

"I'm not hungry," I said.

"I bet they have falafel."

"I'm still not hungry," I said. But I let her pull me to my feet and started trudging through the sand.

TALES OF BRAVE ULYSSES

IT WASN'T LONG BEFORE I BEGAN HEARING OTHER people's voices. Like real people who sounded like they were doing real things. Not trying to eat us. Or kill us. There were kids laughing and crying and songs being sung like some sort of outdoor block party.

Dory led me by the hand, and I trailed along, completely helpless. Sure, I stumbled once or twice. Or maybe five or six times. But I didn't fall once. She was either a really good guide or the ground was pretty even.

"What do you see?" I asked.

"It's a town," Dory said. "With lots of building, like some even two stories high. And we're coming up on some kind of outdoor plaza. And there are a ton of people. Oh! There's a falafel stand."

"Do you see Odysseus?" He could have the scroll. He knew how important it was. He could have it tucked into the belt of his pants. Dory might just not have seen it.

"Not yet, Homer, but we'll keep looking. Are you hungry?"

Even if I were, I didn't see how it would matter. "Do you have any money?" I asked.

"Nope," Dory said. "But I have charm. I'm sure I can get us something to eat."

So, I let Dory drag me to one of the food stands. She positioned me so I could sit up on the barstool. I tried to pretend it was some kind of game, like I was closing my eyes and seeing how much I could do without seeing. Except then I remembered that it wasn't a game. It wasn't fun at all, like games were supposed to be. I really couldn't see. That got me all depressed again.

"Two falafels," Dory said.

"You got any coins?" a guy's voice asked. Not mean or gruff. Just kind of curious and happy because this was a party and he was a part of it.

"Nope," Dory said. "But my friend here will recite you a poem on the spot on a subject of your choosing."

"No, I won't!" I said, because I realized that she was talking about me.

But I guess the guy didn't hear me, or he really wanted a poem because he said. "Sure. How about falafels?"

I shook my head. This was ridiculous. But whatever. Dactylic Hexameter was second nature by now.

Oh I eat / falafels / for lunch and / for breakfast /
each day of / the week
When I have / a mouth of / falafels / so tasty /
I don't want / to speak
Don't ask me / a question / if you see / me chewing /
or you'll break / my mood
You'll find out / you're sorry / when I / have to /
show you / my food
Falafels / are tasty / and crunchy / and crispy /
and simply / divine
Show me a / falafel / and I will / be willing /
to wait in / a line
But don't cook / them wrong / or your / business will /
turn quite / a mess
I'll let the / world know in / one hundred / and forty /
letters / or less

The guy exploded with laughter. "Brilliant! I love it!"

And even though I was depressed, I couldn't help the small smile that crept onto my lips.

"Do you love it enough for two falafels?" Dory asked.

"Today and any other day," the guy said, and pretty soon I felt something being shoved into my hands which was slick with grease and smelled like the Elysian Fields themselves. And despite myself, I took a bite and enjoyed every moment of it.

Maybe this was it. This could be my new life. Dory and

I could live here—wherever here was—and make a living. I could stand on the street corner and recite on-the-spot poems and people could give us money. Dory wouldn't have to be a slave anymore. It was almost brilliant. And since everything else was already lost, there was really nothing more to lose.

"Where are we?" Dory asked, and I made the genius assumption that she wasn't talking to me. Her voice also sounded like her face wasn't looking my way.

"Scherie, rhymes with cheery," the guy said. "Island of the Phaeacians. And you got your timing down right if you just got here. It's Pentathlon time."

"What's Pentathlon?" I asked with a mouth full of falafel. I didn't point out that Scherie also rhymed with dreary.

"What's Pentathlon?" The guy laughed. "You two really are strangers. It's only the biggest competition in the entire world. Athletes and all sorts of people come from all over to compete. And it's only once every five years, so you hit it lucky."

Lucky. Nothing we'd hit so far was lucky. But I decided against arguing with the guy. He did give us free falafels after all.

"Come on," Dory said once we'd finished our falafels. She grabbed at my hand and dragged me off the stool. "Let's go check out the games."

Since I couldn't see, I wasn't going to be doing much checking out of anything, but I let her drag me away. And I'll give Dory this: the entire time we wandered around, she gave me a running account of everything.

According to Dory, there were musicians—yeah, I could

hear these—circus performers, like jugglers and magicians, athletes, and all sorts of stuff. We made our way to a stadium where she said all the sports competitions were going on. And even though I couldn't see, she gave me a second by second narration of who was ahead, who was behind, when someone overtook someone else. She even used funny nicknames for all the people she saw, just like back on the boat. Things like Donut, who she said was a ginormous wrestler, and Zippy, who she said was the fastest sprinter in the world. It made me miss the guys on the ship even more.

"Do you see Odysseus?" I asked. I wanted to make sure she didn't forget that we were looking for him. I still hadn't given up on the scroll. If I could find it, then everything would be almost better.

"Not yet," Dory said. "But the discus throw is starting."

The crowd started chanting out some guy's name, maybe their local champion. "Chopper. Chopper."

I half wanted to join in the chanting, but I couldn't bring myself to do it.

And then Dory said, "Oh! Did you see that?" She cringed and dug her fingernails into my arm.

"Of course, I didn't see it," I said. "I can't see anything."

"Ugh. Homer. Chopper just went to throw the discus, and his arm seriously snapped in half. Snapped in half. Like it was hanging there, wobbling back and forth."

From the way she described it, I was kind of happy I hadn't seen it. Someone within hearing distance threw up, so it must've been pretty gnarly.

"Are there any replacement discus throwers?" the announcer called up through the crowd. "Can anyone take Chopper's place?"

The already restless crowd began to buzz, and then Dory said, "Oh my gods! There's Odysseus. He's taking Chopper's place!"

"You're sure it's him?" I asked, cursing the gods that I couldn't see for myself.

"Yes! It's him. I've spent the last ten years with the guy. I think I recognize him."

"And he's competing?"

"Yes, Homer! The crowd is dragging him forward now. Oh, and that's weird."

"What's weird?" I asked.

"A bunch of the ladies are squeezing his arm muscles. And he's actually smiling about it and waving to the crowd."

Yep. That was our Odysseus. Strong. Buff. A huge fan of the ladies.

Dory started back then on her commentary, using all sorts of measurements to describe to me how far people were throwing the discus. A hippikon. A stadion. A plethron. A milion. I'd heard of all the measurements before, back in school, but they all kind of ran together into way longer than I'd ever be able to throw anything.

And then she smacked me in the arm. Again.

"You need to stop doing that," I said.

"But it's his turn. Homer. And the guy before him threw

really far. There's no way Odysseus can win."

At that I laughed. "You do remember this is Odysseus we're talking about, right?"

"Hmmm … good point," she said.

Then we waited. And held our breath. And finally, after what felt like forever, Dory jumped up to her feet and started cheering, yanking me along next to her.

"He won!" she screamed. "He threw it farther! I can't believe it. He won!"

But I could believe it. This was Odysseus, the hero of my story. Or at least of the story I had been writing. Now I wasn't writing anything. I couldn't see, and I'd lost the scroll. If Odysseus didn't have it, my fate was sealed.

The crowd cheered for a solid ten minutes. Everyone wanted to know who the new mystery discus champion was.

"Can you still see him?" I asked Dory.

"Kind of," she said. "But a bunch of people are pulling him away."

"Don't let him out of your sight," I said.

"I'm not, Homer." Dory grabbed my hand and dragged me from my seat.

I felt myself being yanked into a crowd of people, with everyone shoving along and yammering on about the games, how amazing they were, how they couldn't wait until next time.

"You still see him?" I said.

When Dory didn't say anything, I knew the answer.

"You lost him?" I said.

"People are everywhere, Homer," she said. "But it looks like …"

"Like what?"

"Like everyone's going to the same place."

"Where?" I asked.

She didn't answer. Only stopped. And I felt the crowd rushing past us.

"No way, Homer," Dory said.

"No way what?" I said. "Can we please remember that I can't see a thing here?" My vision was completely white. There was no sign it was ever going to get better.

"The palace," Dory said. "Everyone's going to the palace. And you wouldn't believe this place."

"Tell me," I said.

So, Dory did. She told me how the walls were made of bronze so shiny, they were brighter than the golden cattle of Helios. And how the gate was made of solid gold. And how sitting out front were two giant dogs, bigger than Cerberus, that were crafted of gold and silver that everyone was claiming had been constructed by the god Hephaestus himself. And the rumor was that they came alive at night and protected the place. And as she led me through the gates, she told me about the garden inside which was lined with golden statues holding torches and filled with all sorts of fruit trees.

"I don't believe you," I said, even though I did.

"Wait a second," Dory said, and about ten seconds later, she handed me a piece of fruit.

I bit into it and let the juice run down my face. It tasted like liquid gold on a sunny day. I grinned despite the fact that my life was over. My plan had worked perfectly.

"Okay, what else?" I asked.

"It looks like we're heading toward some sort of amphitheater," Dory said. And she led me onward.

The party was well started. Along with music, some guy was telling a story about the god Ares and the goddess Aphrodite that had way more naughty parts than anything Mom would ever let me hear. But Mom wasn't around to say anything about it. Mom was back in Ionia, hours away from losing everything. The thought brought back my bad mood.

"They say his name is Demodocus," Dory whispered. "Everyone thinks he's amazing."

"Amazing," I said. "I could do way better." Demodocus was trying to use some sort of hexameter but he kept missing or adding beats, making it some mashed up version of pentameter.

At the end of the story, everyone clapped except me. But I guess he didn't need my applause because he burst into a new story. I swallowed hard when I heard what it was about.

"You hear that, Homer?" Dory said, smacking me on the arm.

"Enough on the smacking me," I said.

"But do you hear the story?"

"I'm not deaf," I said, rubbing my arm. Demodocus had launched into a story about of all things, a huge fight between Odysseus and Achilles during the Trojan War. Except when he talked about them, they may as well have been cut out of papyrus because the characters were so flat. He had Odysseus totally wrong, describing him as some weenie wimp while he made Achilles out to be the bravest, strongest guy in the world.

"OMG Homer," Dory said. "Odysseus is here. He's crying."

"Crying? Maybe because the story is so bad."

But the crowd didn't think it was bad at all, and there was a standing ovation once Demodocus was done. And then, once the applause died down, I felt Dory stand up next to me.

"My friend has a story!" she yelled at the top of her lungs.

I yanked at her hand, but she pulled away. She couldn't be serious. No way was I going to get up in front of everyone. No. Way.

But Dory would not shut up. And then a bunch of hands grabbed me and dragged me down a flight of steps, and I knew, with a horrible sick feeling in my stomach, that I was now on the stage in front of everyone.

Soft lyre music started up to my right. I stood there, with no clue what to say. I couldn't do this. Not in front of everyone. Not now, once everything was already lost. Except then I heard Dory's voice somewhere off to the left, nearly inaudible.

"You got this, Homer."

I didn't say anything.

"I believe in you. Believe in yourself."

Don't stop believing.

I'd written it in the margin of the scroll. Maybe I'd written it for myself, because I didn't want to stop believing. I didn't want to lose faith. Not in myself. Not in the world. Not now. Not ever.

And so, I took a deep breath, and I started. I started with the horse. And I crafted the tale of our journey in perfect Dactylic Hexameter. I told of the gloomy island of Ismaros, where the guys got all greedy and raided the place, and how that started our curse from the gods. And then I told about the cyclops. The crowd erupted with laughter at the part where Odysseus told him his name was No One. They also bellowed in frustration that Odysseus would tell the cyclops his real name, so close to our escape. And then I told of Aeolus, the Keeper of the Winds. And of the Laestrygonians. Tears ran down my cheeks as I told of our ships being destroyed. Of so many of the guys dying.

And then I got to the part about Circe and the pigs, and of our visit to the Underworld. And the Sirens and Scylla and Charybdis. And the island of Thrinacia, where the golden cattle were kept. And I told of Polites, making sure everyone knew what a hero he was, and of Eurylochus, making sure if anyone remembered his name, they would know what a rat he'd been. I told of our wrecking on the island of Calypso. Of staying there for seven long years. And how we'd then set out, full of hope, only for our journey to end here. Still not home.

Still not home.

My final words hung in the air.

Silence filled the amphitheater.

And then the crowd erupted with cheers so loud, it sounded like an earthquake. Applause I wouldn't have thought possible. The floor of the stage shook under me.

My throat was so dry, it felt like I'd swallowed sand, and I still couldn't see a thing, but I let some sort of happiness wash over me in that moment. Some semblance of peace.

"But he never got home!" someone from the crowd called once the applause settled down. "Odysseus never completed his journey. You need to finish the story."

I slowly shook my head. "I'm sorry. That's all there is to the story. That's the end."

But the crowd started stomping. And demanding Odysseus get home. And then from amid the chanting cheers, another voice called out. A voice I'd heard every single day for the last ten years.

"I'm Odysseus."

And that's when the crowd took over. They recognized him as the mysterious discus throwing champion, which only added to their fervor. The king of this place, Alcinous was his name, declared that the Phaeacians would carry Odysseus back to Ithaca in a ship of their own. That they were the most skilled mariners in the entire world. And as they planned the entire thing, Dory pulled me off the stage and somewhere away from the crowd.

She shoved something into my hand.

"I wrote it all down, Homer."

"Wrote what all down?" I asked.

"Your story. Every single word. I wrote it all down. And yes, before you say it, I know that this isn't your precious scroll, but it's still the story. And when we get back to Ionia, you can make sure that's good enough."

My story.

Back to Ionia.

My future.

Without thinking, I grabbed Dory in a giant hug. "You are the best friend in the entire world. You know that, right?"

"You're crushing me, Homer," she said.

"I don't care. Did you hear me? There has never been anyone who's been a better friend than you."

"Okay. Okay. You're welcome," she said. "Now, let me go."

So, I did, but not before giving her one final hug. Dory was the best part of this entire journey.

"We're going to get home, Homer," Dory said.

I squeezed her hand. "Yep. We're going to get home."

A Farewell to Kings

THE PHAEACIANS WEREN'T KIDDING ABOUT HAVING a thing for boats. According the Dory, the harbor they took us to was filled with at least one hundred ships of all sizes, colors, and shapes. She even claimed there was one shaped like a giant hippopotamus, though I'm not sure I believed her. She could've just been trying to make me smile. But I didn't need a hippopotamus boat to make me smile. We were actually going to get home.

"How much time is left in the hourglass?" I asked. I hated this not seeing anything stuff. I had to ask about everything.

"Maybe a day," she said.

"Not to worry, Bard," Odysseus said. "When we reach my homeland of Ithaca, I'll be welcomed with open arms. My countrymen will take you by ship to your home of Ionia."

I didn't want to go anywhere in a ship with anyone that had even the smallest bit to do with Odysseus, but I smiled and nodded like it was a perfect plan.

"Aboard!" someone said.

"That's the captain," Dory whispered to me.

We trundled aboard, Dory leading me.

"Where are the oars?" Odysseus said.

"No oars," the captain said. He was a hulking guy with a shaved head, a bare chest, and enough muscles to give Odysseus a run for his money.

"What kind of lunacy is that?" Odysseus said. "By the gods. We'll get nowhere on a ship like this."

He didn't sound angry. Just discouraged. Like once again, we were so close, only to fail one more time.

"The lunacy of magic," the captain said. "Our ships don't need oars. They sail by the—"

"If you say by the power of the gods, I am out of here," Odysseus said.

The captain laughed, a deep, hearty sound that boomed around in his chest. "Not by the power of the gods. By pure and simple thought."

"Thought?" I said, trying to commit the conversation to memory. I could recite it to Dory later, and hopefully she'd agree to keep writing it down.

"Thought," the captain said. "Dream of your homeland. Dream of it, and the ship will take us there."

Odysseus made a couple garbled noises in his throat, but

then we continued aboard. And the next thing I knew, he was snoring louder than I'd ever heard him snore before. Or maybe my hearing was getting better since I couldn't see. But no sooner did his snores fill the air around us, the ship leapt forward.

"Have you thought of a title?" Dory asked next to me.

"A title for what?" I said.

"Duh, Homer. Your story," Dory said. "You need a title."

A title couldn't hurt. Maybe it would even get me extra credit. So, I spent the better part of the next hour, tossing possibilities around in my mind.

"I got it," I finally said.

"Got what?" Dory asked, yawning. We were both having a pretty hard time staying awake.

"The title," I said.

"Oh. What is it?"

"*Homer's Immortal Index of Opus Deities.*" I said it with confidence since it was such a masterful achievement. Alliteration. Cleverness. An homage to the gods. My title had it all.

"*Homer's … Immortal … Index …*"

"*Of Opus Deities,*" I finished for her. It wasn't that hard to remember once you got the hang of it.

"It's a little long," Dory said.

"It's epic."

"And long," Dory said. "You need something shorter."

"Like what? *Homer?*" Which wasn't such a bad idea. Naming a story after myself, as the author, felt kind of awesome.

"How about *The Odyssey?*" Dory said.

"*The Odyssey?*"

"Sure. It's short. Sweet. Easy to remember."

"It's boring." I tried to consider her words and open my mind to possibilities. Maybe my title was too long. Maybe I should listen to feedback more often. "How about *Homer's Excellent Adventure?*" I finally said.

Dory opened her mouth like she was sounding it out. I was sure she was trying to find a flaw with it. But instead she said, "*Homer's Excellent Adventure.* It's perfect."

And so, I had a title.

I guess I fell asleep after that, because brainstorming was really hard work, and the ship had gone quiet. The next thing I knew, Dory was shaking me awake.

"We're here," she said.

I rubbed my eyes, but I couldn't see even the brightness of the day.

"I can't see the sun," I said.

"It's nighttime," Dory said. "And we made it to Ithaca. I see the same crest from the sails on the flags here. And everything's really rocky, just like Odysseus said. But there's this path that leads from the shore."

She led me off the ship because I didn't want to fall into the water and have Poseidon swallow me whole. And maybe I should have felt differently, now that we'd reached Odysseus' homeland, except it was his homeland, not mine. His journey may be over, but mine and Dory's still wasn't.

"How I wish my eyes could look upon my homeland and

know that all was well," Odysseus said, and heaviness filled his voice. "But this forebodes danger."

"What forebodes danger?" I asked Dory, under my breath.

"There's no one here to meet him," Dory said. "Not his wife. Not his servants. Not his son. No one."

"Why?" I asked. "Where are they?"

She leaned close. "One of our sailors heard that there's a bunch of guys trying to become king. They all think Odysseus is dead."

"So, he should just tell people he's not dead," I said. It seemed really simple and straightforward, unlike anything else that had gone on so far in his story.

Just then, I felt a hand clasp me on the shoulder.

"That I cannot do," Odysseus said. "If this journey that we've shared has taught me one thing, it's that I must proceed with caution. Otherwise, everything I've learned in our travels, the death of my mother, being away from my homeland for so long … all of it will be for naught."

Wow. Just wow. Maybe after all these years, Odysseus really had changed. Maybe this is what Elder Pachis had meant when he told me about character growth. Odysseus was a way different person than he'd been ten years ago when we'd met him.

"Bard, you've done me a great service," Odysseus said. "And I wish I could repay you by taking you to your homeland this very moment. But …"

Yeah. Yeah. I knew how the rest of that sentence was going to go. He was home, finally, and he couldn't leave. At least not until things were settled. His story was over.

Ours? Not so much. We still needed to get back within the next few hours or our time would run out.

But Odysseus didn't stand there and make a bunch of excuses. He told us the situation, he promised he would help when he'd secured the throne once again, and then he bade us farewell.

"Bard, I am eternally in your debt," he said. And then he clasped me in a hug and turned away, leaving us there, on the shore.

"It's okay," I said to Dory because I couldn't change Odysseus' story. He had his responsibilities, and I had mine. "Maybe the Phaeacians will take us."

"The Phaeacians are gone already," Dory said.

"Gone? Seriously? What? Has it been a whole five minutes? They couldn't wait around longer than that?"

"They didn't want to risk the wrath of Poseidon," Dory said.

"Well, that's just perfect," I said. "We have the worst luck ever."

"Yeah, maybe," Dory said.

I let her grab my arm and drag me forward. And since no one cared who we were, no one stopped us on our way to the city center.

The sun was just coming up as we walked because light began to fill in my empty vision. And soon, the sounds of people and civilization reached my ears once again.

"You hungry, Homer?" Dory asked.

"No," I said.

She ignored my pouting and plunked me down on a stool somewhere in the middle of town.

"We'll take breakfast," Dory said.

"Breakfast!" the guy who must've run the food cart said. "I got something better for you."

And he set something down on the bar in front of me, and the center of my vision began to clear, just the smallest amount, like I could see through a fuzzy murky tunnel.

"Homer …," Dory said.

"I see it," I said. And then I reached out and grabbed it. It was a small wooden horse, like a child's toy. A horse I'd seen before, almost in a different lifetime. And on the side of the horse was a small door, held closed by a latch.

I used my thumb to push the latch open. And then we were sucked through.

THE MARK IS THE SECRET

WE ENDED UP BACK AT THE FALAFEL STAND. THE one in Ionia, that is. My vision was still really blurry and narrow, like I was looking down a long tunnel, but I could see shapes now, like shadows. I felt next to me. Dory wasn't there.

"Dory?"

"Right here, Homer," she said.

I could barely make out her shape in the bright tunnel of my vision. She was across the bar, like she was running the stand.

Like she'd been running the stand when we left on the journey.

The wooden horse sat on the counter between us.

"Um …" My hand still rested on the horse, but I pulled it back as fast as I could.

"Um …," Dory agreed.

262

"What just happened?" I asked. The world slowly filled in around me. Or maybe it wasn't so much the world as my memories, slipping back into the places they'd been ten years ago.

Ten years ago. That didn't even seem possible.

"The hourglass," I said, fumbling under my shirt to find it. "How much sand is left?"

Dory grabbed the rope that hung around my neck and pulled out the hourglass.

"Not good, Homer," she said.

I couldn't see the details of the sand. My vision was still too blurry.

"How much time?"

She pushed it in front of my eyes. "Only a couple grains of sand are left."

A couple grains of sand. That wasn't good at all.

"Come on," I said, and I jumped from the bar stool. But then I tripped on something because I couldn't see more than a foot away. I landed hard on my knees, jamming the flats of my hands into the unforgiving stone ground.

"Careful, Homer," Dory said, and she grabbed the horse from the counter and came around to help me up.

"I need to get to the school," I said. "Before time runs out."

And so we ran, Dory holding my hand and guiding me around whatever or whoever happened to get in our way. I think we knocked into people and ran into a few vegetable carts because some of the town people started yelling at us. Each step we took, the worry growing inside me built up. I could not run out of time now. Not when we were so close. Not when we'd been through so much.

It was only seconds before we were on the outskirts of town, where the barn-turned-school sat in the middle of the field, but it felt like a month. A year. My entire sense of time was gone. The dull white walls reflected the sun, making my already white-washed vision a renewed cloud of brilliant nothing. But Dory kept hold of me and pulled me forward. It was only when we got right up to the door that she finally stopped.

"What are you doing?" I said. Every second counted.

"I can't go inside, Homer," Dory said.

"Of course, you can," I said. "I can't see without you."

"No," Dory said. "You forget …"

"Forget what?"

She blew out a deep breath. "You forget I'm a slave, Homer. And slaves can't go into schools. It's against the law."

That had to be the most ridiculous thing I'd ever heard. After everything. Dory should be able to go anywhere I could. There was nothing that set us apart.

"Don't worry," I said. "No one will know."

"They'll know," she said.

"But I need you."

The seconds ticked by. The precious seconds that we almost didn't have. And then, even though I didn't even believe my own words, Dory, to her credit, led me inside.

Elder Pachis was yammering on about something up at the front of the classroom. At least one person was snoring.

I couldn't tell who since I couldn't see hardly at all. But the second we stepped inside, he stopped talking. The snoring continued.

"Homer," Elder Pachis said. "This isn't your school anymore. You need to leave."

I stepped forward and reached for the scroll inside my tunic.

"I got the story," I said, and I pulled out the scroll. "I finished the project."

He made an annoying clucking sound with his tongue. "It's too late. You're out of time."

My head snapped to Dory. We could not be out of time. But my limited tunnel vision was enough to show me that she was nodding her head, super slowly. She held the hourglass in one hand.

Out of time.

No. I was not going to accept that.

I pulled my hand from Dory's and stepped forward, weaving around what I hoped were all the benches. The last thing I needed to do here was trip on something and have any hopes of me looking halfway cool crumble.

"I got your story. Just like you said." And then I let the scroll unroll in front of me.

By now the entire class was listening. Whoever was snoring had stopped.

Then Demetrios said, "Just leave already, Homer. Go pack your things. My dad—the mayor—is taking over your farm today."

That was not happening. But I wasn't going to get into some pointless bickering match with Demetrios. Not now. Not ever.

"It's late," Elder Pachis said, but his voice didn't sound quite as convinced as it had only a minute ago.

"It's everything you wanted." I was not backing down.

I took another step forward. So did he. And I guess that's when he saw the scroll.

"It's not the right scroll," Elder Pachis said.

"True," I said. "But that scroll was lost at sea. Swallowed by the monster Charybdis. A most heinous creature."

"What's Charybdis?" someone asked. I was pretty sure it was Lysandra, but I didn't turn to look. Not like I'd have been able to see more than a foot, anyway.

"A terrible sea monster," I said. "Destroyer of ships and men. The scroll tells all about it."

"It does?" Elder Pachis said, and then he stepped forward again.

"It does," I said. "In perfectly measured Dactylic Hexameter."

I guess this last part got him because he leaned forward and craned his head so he could begin to read. And then he took the scroll in his hands and held it all proper and started to say the words aloud. And I listened as he read the stanzas and tasted the words on his lips. And it was funny, hearing my story from someone else. It was actually good. Really, really good. Way better than I'd even thought.

Time slipped by as Elder Pachis read my story, becoming more animated as the story went on, almost like the poetry demanded attention. And in that time, I felt Dory creep up behind me.

Finally, Elder Pachis said, "Homer."

I swallowed the lump that had been stuck in my throat since we got to the school.

"Yeah?"

"You did it," Elder Pachis said. "You came up with a story of epic proportion."

"I know," is what I wanted to say, but in the last ten years, I'd learned that maybe a witty sarcastic response isn't always the best choice. So, what I said aloud was, "Thank you."

"This will work," Elder Pachis said.

"I can stay in school?"

"You can stay in school."

I almost asked if I could still be a soldier, but even if I could see, now I wasn't so sure that was what I wanted. Not anymore.

"The farm is still ours?" I asked instead.

"The farm is still yours," Elder Pachis said.

"No way!" Demetrios said. "That farm is mine now. And you and your mom need to leave today or we're going to kick you out."

"You're not kicking Homer out," Dory said, stepping up next to me.

"Shut up, slave," Demetrios said. "Why is there a slave in the classroom, anyway? That's against the law."

Dory opened her mouth and started to say something, but I cut her off.

267

"Don't talk to her that way," I said. And then I kind of cringed because I'd completely used the wrong pronoun. Or at least the right pronoun, but the one I shouldn't have used.

"*She*," Demetrios said, enunciating it, "is a slave. *She* belongs to my family."

I tried to stare Demetrios down, because he was such a jerk, but he was too far away for me to really see. My tunnel vision narrowed the more I tried, and the more I tried, the more it hurt my eyes.

I whipped back around to Elder Pachis, and I opened my mouth to say something, except then I forgot what it was because my vision narrowed even more until all I could see was one tiny circle pinpoint of light, focused on the wall above Elder Pachis' head.

There, on the wall of the reclaimed barn, was a seal. A seal with a symbol I'd seen before.

The siren's song came back to me.

"*Look to the seal.*"

"*The seal is the answer.*"

"*The seal will set her free.*"

And then Old Lady Tessa's words came back to me.

"*The mark is the secret.*"

Just like the mark on Dory's neck. The tattoo.

"What is that?" I pointed to the spot on the wall. It widened in my vision.

Elder Pachis turned to look where I pointed. "What?"

"That mark. On the wall."

"Oh, that," he said. "It's the ancient seal of the royal family."

"The royal family is dying out," Demetrios said. "When Ajax died, it was all over for them. Once King Telamon kicks the bucket, my dad'll be king." He kept yammering, something about what a great job his dad was doing of being mayor of Ionia, but I stopped listening to him.

"The family of Ajax. That's it." It was the same king. It was no coincidence that we'd met Ajax. That we'd heard his story. Or that he'd talked to Dory in the Underworld.

"What's it, Homer?" Elder Pachis said.

"The line of Ajax," I said. "It's not gone."

"Is to," Demetrios said.

"Wrong," I said. "Because this girl you see before you—yes, she's a girl. That part kind of surprised me, too, except then I spent ten years with her, and there is no mistaking it—is actually the daughter of Ajax, hero of the Trojan War. If I remember my history of Ionia correctly—and I'm pretty sure I do since I was listening in class that day—King Telamon gave his son Ajax this land to rule over. But then your family took over when you thought he had died."

"He had died," Demetrios said, fumbling over his words.

"Maybe so," I said. "But he left a child. A daughter, fathered during the war. Stowed away on a Greek ship after the war to be returned safely here. Not to be forced into slavery."

"But … but that's not possible," Demetrios said. "You don't have any proof of that."

"Of course, I do," I said. "You don't think the gods just leave this stuff up to chance, do you?"

"What proof?" Demetrios said.

"Dory?" I craned my neck in her direction, even though I still was having trouble making out complete shapes. And I definitely couldn't see faces.

"What Homer?" she said.

"Show your tattoo."

Her hand went to her neck.

"No, Homer," she said, keeping it hidden like she always did.

"You have to," I said. "The mark is the secret. That's what Tessa told me. It's the proof. It will set you free."

Dory took a deep breath, like she was ready to jump off the side of a cliff, and then she pulled her hair from off the back of her neck. And even though I couldn't see the tattoo, I was sure everyone else in the classroom could because the entire group let out an audible gasp.

"The crest of the king's family," I said. "Put there by Ajax and the gods after her birth. And what do you think King Telamon will say when he finds out that your family has kept his granddaughter as a slave for the last ten years?"

"Oh crud," Demetrios said, and he ran from the school, maybe to warn his dad.

I guess Elder Pachis believed what I said, because he started making a huge deal about Dory, making sure she had the best seat near the front of the classroom, even brushing off the dirt and hay from the bench himself. He hadn't cleared off a space for me, but I shoved myself in there next to Dory, and then

Elder Pachis returned to the front of the room and started lecturing again.

And that's how Dory went from being a slave to becoming the rightful heir of Ionia.

This Is the End

So that's how our story ends. Dory got reunited with her family. There was all sorts of ceremony and celebration. King Telamon threw a weeklong feast. Then he wanted her to move back to the palace, but she insisted she wasn't leaving Ionia since she'd be ruling it someday, so she moved into a fancy house with a bunch of servants—not slaves; she vowed to free all of them—not too far from the farm. I gave her one of the cats from our farm as a housewarming present. She named it Grumpy.

As for the farm, Mom and I got to keep it. Actually own the farm forever, like no chance it could ever be taken away from us. That was a nice benefit of being best friends with the king's granddaughter.

And Demetrios? Let's just say that his family was relieved

of all their responsibilities around town. Sure, he was still allowed to come to school, but he sat in the back and moped the entire time. He even had to scrub pig dung off the walls. I didn't miss his bullying once. Oh yeah, and Lysandra dumped him hard. In front of everyone. Totally embarrassing.

Each day my vision got a little bit better. Still not perfect, and I had to have Dory help me with my writing.

Yeah, I kept writing. Now that I'd figured out how much I loved it, I couldn't let it go. Not now. Not ever. My destiny was not to be a soldier after all. Charon was right about that.

One day, about a month later, I sat at the falafel stand. Dory still ran the thing after school. She insisted on it, no matter how much her grandpa—the king—insisted it wasn't proper for royalty. But Dory wasn't about to start listening to authority now.

"What'cha writing about, Homer?" she asked. This was the fifth day in a row she'd asked the same question.

I traced my pen along the scroll. What I was writing was a whole bunch of nothing. For the last week, I'd completely run out of ideas.

"I don't know," I said. "Falafels?"

"Falafels don't make very good stories. Their insides can get kind of soggy."

I picked at my food, wishing there was some deep inspiration hidden inside, because writer's block sucked. But the ideas just wouldn't come, and it seemed like the harder I thought about them, the more they stayed away.

"I need a story idea," I said.

"Story ideas are everywhere," someone said next to me.

I looked over, and there was none other than Hermes himself, sitting on the exact same bench he'd been on ten years ago. Or I guess it was only a month and ten days ago. The gods made everything confusing.

"Easy for you to say," I said.

"It's true," Hermes said. "For example, did you know that your friend Dory here, her grandfather, none other than King Telamon himself ..." His words trailed off.

"My grandfather what?" Dory said.

Hermes shook his head, and the wings on his hat fluttered back and forth. "Nothing. It's nothing."

"Tell me," Dory said.

"No," Hermes said. "You two are probably sick of adventures."

I glanced to Dory, who got a really funny grin on her face. A grin that probably matched my own.

"Why don't you test us?" I said. "What about King Telamon?"

Hermes pulled something from the bag he wore slung around his shoulder and set it on the counter in front of us. It was a miniature model of a ship. Not a ship like Odysseus had. Not like the Phaeacians either. This ship was long and sleek and looked like it could slip through the water almost in stealth mode.

"Well, I didn't see it with my own eyes, but rumors have it

that King Telamon himself actually traveled with none other than Jason himself."

"Jason who?" I asked.

Hermes grinned. "Do you want to find out?"

GLOSSARY

GODS AND IMMORTAL-ISH BEINGS

ATHENA — Greek goddess of wisdom, war, inspiration and courage; of the Greek gods, she is the biggest supporter of Odysseus; loves owls

HERMES — Greek messenger god; can pass between the worlds of the living and the dead; wears an awesome hat with wings on it

ZEUS — King of the Greek gods; god of the sky; carries around a mean thunderbolt which he's not afraid to use

POSEIDON — Greek god of the sea; Earth-shaker; dad of the cyclops; a real pain in Odysseus' backside.

POLYPHEMUS — a giant cyclops; the son of Poseidon; favorite hobbies include eating men for lunch and eating men for dinner; also eating men for breakfast

AEOLUS — keeper of the winds; lives on the floating island of Aeolia; has twelve sons and daughters; loves to hear stories

BETA — an early reader of Homer's story; daughter of Aeolus

276

THE TWELVE CHILDREN OF AEOLUS — Alpha, Beta, Gamma, Delta, Epsilon, Digamma, Zeta, Eta, Theta, Iota, Kappa, Lambda

CIRCE — a powerful sorceress who lives on the island of Aeaea; possibly the daughter of Helios; often turned her enemies or those who offended her into animals; don't offend her

CHARON — the creepy ferryman who shuttles dead people across the River Styx into the Underworld

TIRESIAS — a prophet of the Greek god Apollo; dead and now resides in the Underworld; transformed into a woman for seven years (which isn't relevant but is interesting)

SIRENS — three killer mermaids; used to be best friends with Persephone before she was taken away to the Underworld; sing songs to make men jump to their death

SCYLLA — a terrifying monster with six heads; she always strikes at least once

CHARYBDIS — an equally terrifying monster who lives under the sea and creates a whirlpool to suck down anything that crosses her path

HELIOS — Greek Titan; personification of the sun; has an island where his golden cattle live; still undetermined if the cattle produce golden milk

CALYPSO — a sea nymph who lives alone on the island of Ogygia; possibly the daughter of the Titan Atlas; fell in love with Odysseus and wanted him to stay with her forever and ever and ever

PEOPLE

HOMER — the main character of our story; also the fabled poet/author of *The Odyssey* and *The Iliad*

ODYSSEUS — a Greek hero during the Trojan War; King of Ithaca; the genius behind the Trojan Horse

DORY (DORYCLUS) — Homer's best friend; a slave from Ionia

ELDER PACHIS — Homer's teacher back in Ionia

DEMETRIOS — an irritating kid at Homer's school back in Ionia; son of the mayor of Ionia

LYSANDRA — a cute girl from Homer's school back in Ionia

POLITES — Odysseus' shipmate and dearest friend

EURYLOCHUS — a relative of Odysseus through marriage; annoys the heck out of Odysseus

CICONES — the people of the island of Ismaros

OLD LADY TESSA — a (possible) witch who lives on the island of Ismaros; likes poetry

THE FLOWER CHILDREN — the people of the Island of the Lotus Eaters

LAESTRYGONIANS — the people of the Island of Lamos; they also happen to be cannibals

ELPENOR — one of Odysseus' men who fell off a roof and died

PHAEACIANS — the people of the island of Scherie

DEMODOCUS — storyteller from the Phaeacian Pentathlon

KING ALCINOUS — King of the Phaeacians

PENELOPE — Odysseus' wife; possibly the most patient woman in the world

TELEMACHUS — Odysseus' son; newborn when Odysseus set out for the Trojan War

KING TELAMON — King of Ionia

AJAX — son of King Telamon; Greek hero from the Trojan War

HELEN — the woman held responsible for starting the Trojan War

OTHER GUYS ON THE SHIPS — Fish, The Guy Who Hangs out with Fish, Cupcake, Spitter, Rum, Moronios, Pork, Ear, Skinner, Tailor, Lefty

OTHER PEOPLE FROM THE TROJAN WAR — Agamemnon, Nestor, Peisistratus, Menelaus, Achilles, Cassandra, Clytemnestra

PLACES

ITHACA — the island where Odysseus is king

IONIA — Homer's homeland

TROY—the place where the ten-year-long Trojan War between the Trojans and the Spartans happened; the Trojans didn't win

ISMAROS — the island of the Cicones

THE ISLAND OF THE LOTUS EATERS — where the Flower Children live

AEOLIA — the floating island of Aeolus

LAMOS — the island of the Laestrygonians

TELEPYLUS — the city of the Laestrygonians

AEAEA — the island of Circe

THE UNDERWORLD — where all the dead people go

RIVER STYX — the river in the Underworld that all the dead people entering must cross

THRINACIA — the island of Helios where the sacred golden cattle are kept

OGYGIA — the island of Calypso

SCHERIE — rhymes with cheery (also dreary); the island of the Phaeacians

THINGS

TROJAN HORSE — the huge wooden horse that Odysseus and his men hid inside to sneak into the city of Troy; helped win the war

TROJAN WAR — a crazy ten-year-long war started because some Trojan prince named Paris stole Helen, the wife of the Spartan king Menelaus

THE SCROLL — the piece of papyrus that Homer recorded his story on; respect the Scroll

DACTYLIC HEXAMETER — a pretty cool form of poetry; see "HOMER'S SUPER SIMPLE GUIDE TO DACTYLIC HEXAMETER" for more information

MEAD — a really gross old-person drink; not recommended

HOLY MOLY — the herb given to Odysseus by Hermes to keep him from falling under Circe's spell

PENTATHLON — a contest featuring five events

MAP

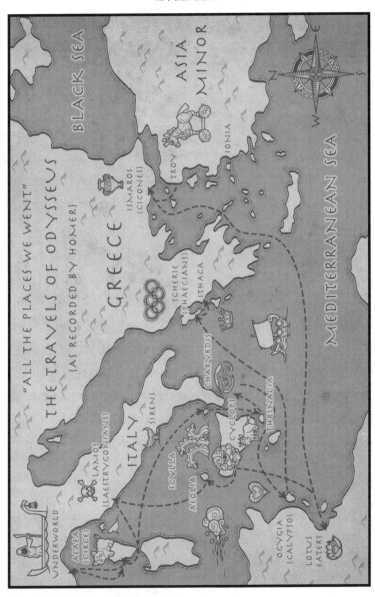

HOMER'S SUPER SIMPLE GUIDE TO DACTYLIC HEXAMETER

WANT TO IMPRESS YOUR TEACHERS? MAKE ALL your friends gaze at you with awe? Have your name remembered for thousands of years to come? Here's my suggestion. Learn Dactylic Hexameter. No, really. It's nowhere near as hard as you think. All you have to do is figure out what you want to say and learn to be a little bit clever about how you say it.

HERE'S THE SCOOP. DACTYLIC HEXAMETER IS ALL about syllables. Kind of like Haiku except way cooler. There are some terms you might want to know. You don't need to remember their names, but this guide would feel way incomplete without them. But don't let them scare you just because you've never seen them before. They're just words, not monsters. Monsters are scary. Words? Not so much.

METER – the type of rhyming scheme you're using, made up of a bunch of lines. In our case, the meter is Dactylic Hexameter, but this is just one of many different types of meter. You can check those others out on your own.

284

FOOT – this is like a section of a line. Since the meter we're working in is hexameter, there are six of these feet in one line.

DACTYL – a foot made up of one long and two short syllables (so three syllables in total)

SPONDEE – a foot made up of two long syllables (so two syllables in total)

WHAT'S A LONG SYLLABLE? WHAT'S A SHORT SYLlable? I wouldn't get too caught up in worrying about that. For now, get the general rules down, and then later, once you're a master, you can worry about things like diphthongs.

GENERAL RULES TO FOLLOW:
   1) The sixth foot should be a spondee.
   2) The fifth foot should be a dactyl if possible (but not required).
   3) The first through fourth feet can be spondees or dactyls.

Yep. That's it. Three simple rules. Anyone can do it.

Check out the cool picture on the next page I drew to show you what I'm talking about.

Here are some of my favorite examples of Dactylic Hexameter.

Your feet are | so smelly | they make me | feel queasy |
so I plug | my nose.

Pancakes | and waffles | with syrup | and sugar |
are always | so nice.

School is | so boring | and makes me | so sleepy |
sometimes my | eyes close.

Potatoes | are lumpy | and ugly | but French fries |
are simply | divine.

Go ahead. Try some of your own. Challenge your friends to see who can up with the funniest, most clever line of meter ever.

286

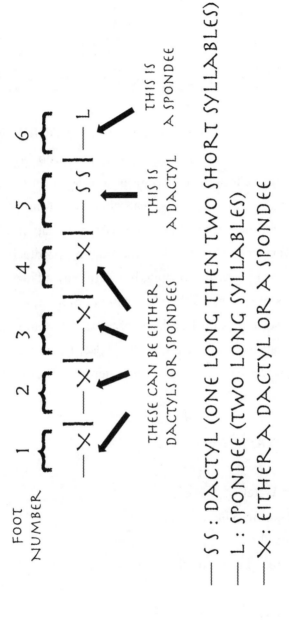

FOOT NUMBER

1 2 3 4 5 6

THESE CAN BE EITHER
DACTYLS OR SPONDEES

THIS IS
A DACTYL

THIS IS
A SPONDEE

— S S : DACTYL (ONE LONG THEN TWO SHORT SYLLABLES)
— L : SPONDEE (TWO LONG SYLLABLES)
— X : EITHER A DACTYL OR A SPONDEE

DORY'S RECIPES: THE TASTIEST HARDTACK IN THE (ANCIENT) WORLD

AFTER READING ABOUT ALL OUR STRUGGLES ON board the ship with finding food, you're probably worried about having enough stocked away in case of an emergency. And though canned food is great when your tummy is rumbling, sometimes you want some variety. To that end, I wrote down every step Dory took while making hardtack. It may seem kind of gross and boring, but here's my advice. Make it now and store it away. When you run out of food, you'll thank me. This stuff lasts for hundreds of years. Oh, and make sure your dental insurance is up to date. Also, if you wear braces, you might want to soak it in some water first. They don't call it hardtack for nothing.

THINGS YOU'LL NEED:

1 cup Water
2 teaspoons Salt
3 cups Flour
A spatula, knife, cookie sheet, bowl, and nail

WHAT TO DO:

Set your oven for 375°F (190°C). You probably want to check with an adult before doing this since 375°F (190°C) is pretty hot.

Mix the flour and salt together. Then mix in the water slowly, mushing it with your hands to blend it all together. Make sure to wash your hands first because otherwise, that's just gross.

Once it's all mixed together, flatten it out until it's about half an inch thick. (That's about as thick as your finger.)

Make a bunch of holes in it with a nail (a clean nail, not a rusty one that you pulled out of your fence).

Use a knife to cut it into rectangles of whatever size you want the servings to be. Place these pieces on a cookie sheet.

Stick the cookie sheet in the oven for 30 minutes. Take it out. Use a spatula to flip over the pieces.

Stick it back in the oven for another 30 minutes. Hopefully by now it's golden brown.

Take the cookie sheet out of the oven. As much as I know you want to dig right in, let the pieces cool for at least 30 minutes because they get kind of hot.

ENJOY! AND WATCH YOUR TEETH.

ABOUT THE AUTHOR

P. J. (TRICIA) HOOVER WANTED TO BE A JEDI, BUT when that didn't work out, she became an electrical engineer instead. After a fifteen year bout designing computer chips for a living, P. J. started creating worlds of her own. She's the award-winning author of *The Hidden Code*, a *Da Vinci Code*-style young adult adventure with a kick-butt heroine, and *Tut: The Story of My Immortal Life*, featuring a fourteen-year-old King Tut who's stuck in middle school. When not writing, P. J. spends time practicing kung fu, solving Rubik's cubes, and watching Star Trek. For more information about P. J. (Tricia) Hoover, please visit her website www.pjhoover.com.